"I'm going to appoint a new trainer for you, Joseph."

"If you don't continue as my trainer, Connie, I'll leave. I can't blame you for not wanting to work with me, but I don't want anyone else."

"But you're not ready to leave yet," she protested. "I don't want you to lose all you've gained."

Joseph laid his hand on her shoulder. "When I sat on that bench this morning after my jog, exhausted, and you were holding my hand, I realized how bleak my life has been for the past year, and I compared it to the serenity and peace I have with you. I don't know what the future holds for us, but I can't let you go out of my life completely, and that's what will happen if I leave here."

Connie swallowed a sob, and moved closer to him....

Books by Irene Brand

Love Inspired

Child of Her Heart #19
Heiress #37
To Love and Honor #49
A Groom To Come Home To #70
Tender Love #95
The Test of Love #114

IRENE BRAND

This prolific and popular author of both contemporary and historical inspirational fiction is a native of West Virginia, where she has lived all her life. She began writing professionally in 1977, after she completed her master's degree in history at Marshall University. Irene taught in secondary public schools for twenty-three years, but retired in 1989 to devote herself full-time to her writing.

In 1984, after she had enjoyed a long career of publishing articles and devotional materials, her first novel was published by Thomas Nelson. Since that time, Irene has published twenty-one contemporary and historical novels and three nonfiction titles with publishers such as Zondervan, Fleming Revell and Barbour Books.

Her extensive travels with her husband, Rod, to forty-nine of the United States and thirty-two foreign countries, have inspired much of her writing. Through her writing, Irene believes she has been helpful to others and is grateful to the many readers who have written to say that her truly inspiring stories and compelling portrayals of characters of strong faith have made a positive impression on their lives. You can write to her at P.O. Box 2770, Southside, WV 25187.

The Test of Love
Irene Brand

Love Inspired®

Published by Steeple Hill Books™

STEEPLE HILL BOOKS

Steeple Hill™

ISBN 0-373-87120-1

THE TEST OF LOVE

Copyright © 2000 by Irene B. Brand

Visit us at www.steeplehill.com

Printed in U.S.A.

Do you not know that your body is a temple of the Holy Spirit, who is in you, whom you have received from God? You are not your own; you were bought at a price. Therefore honor God with your body.

—I Corinthians 6:19-20

Chapter One

A snatch of song marked Connie Harmon's progress as she jogged slowly along the driveway and into the New Life Center's administration building. A tall, slender brunette, she bubbled with vigor and vitality. Most of her life, Connie's gaiety had been spontaneous, but events of the past few months had dampened her spirits, and at times she'd had to force her cheerfulness. The chorus she sang today, "In my heart there rings a melody," didn't always reflect her true emotional state.

Before going down the hallway to her office, Connie paused in front of the foyer's wide expanse of windows to gaze at a scene that never failed to soothe and inspire her. Brilliant snowbanks clung to the peaks of the Rocky Mountains several miles to the southwest, while on the lawn, a robin stiffened its legs and tugged purposefully on a worm in the row of yellow tulips, which were frosted by early-morning dew.

Continuing toward the reception room, Connie sang the refrain of "When It's Springtime in the Rockies," in her pleasing, soprano voice, attempting to keep her spirits high. She was scheduled to discuss monthly bills and accounts with her secretary, Kim Watson, and since her financial condition was usually discouraging, she wanted to get the task behind her.

Connie owned the New Life Center near Idaho Springs, in one of Colorado's oldest historic districts. And though she operated on a hand-to-mouth budget, her financial condition was better than it had been when she'd opened the Center three years ago. Her college degree in physical therapy and psychology hadn't equipped her to be an administrator—she'd had to learn that on her own, and it had been rough.

The phone rang as Connie walked in the door. She waved to Kim and moved toward the adjacent office, but the receptionist stopped Connie with an imperious shake of her head as she picked up the phone. Connie's large blue eyes glimmered with amusement at Kim's gesture, and her sensitive, well-formed mouth broke into a grin that spread over her finely chiseled features. Who was boss here anyway? But she and Kim had been best friends for years, and Connie was used to Kim ordering her around. So perched on the edge of the desk, she waited until Kim answered a query from a local boy about their gymnastic equipment.

Kim replaced the phone, her brown eyes flashing a message Connie couldn't decipher until she scanned the note Kim scribbled on a scrap of paper. "A visitor is waiting in your office."

Connie lifted her eyebrows, and Kim wrote, "Joseph Caldwell."

"*The* Joseph Caldwell?" Connie mouthed silently. Kim nodded, and Connie said quietly, "Why?"

The receptionist shook her head and wrote again. "He said that it was very important that he see you today, and he wouldn't take, no, for an answer."

What could Joseph Caldwell want so urgently from NLC? A well-known Colorado rancher, Caldwell often appeared on television as a spokesman for legislation to promote the rural interests of the state. Occasionally, he'd been a featured rider in rodeos at the state fair, and although she'd never seen him in person, whenever Connie saw him on television, she'd had the urge to learn more about him. Regardless of why he'd come today, Connie looked forward to meeting him.

When she entered her office, the man sitting in the visitor's chair rose with effort and leaned on his cane. He was dressed in a tailored denim suit, a blue-plaid shirt and cowboy boots. A wide-brimmed white hat lay on a chair beside him.

Her visitor was a man of medium height, only a couple of inches taller than Connie, but he had broad shoulders and handled himself with dignity. His hair was light-brown, and steely gray eyes glistened above his high cheekbones. A wide, determined mouth and a straight nose indicated his strength of character.

"I'm Joseph Caldwell," he said slowly, almost with a drawl.

Joseph Caldwell in the flesh was even more appealing than he appeared on TV, and with downcast eyes, Connie's fingers fumbled with the papers on her desk, fearful that her visitor would detect her sudden interest. She'd heard it said that following a broken relationship, a person was apt to rebound quickly into another's arms, and at the moment, Joseph's arms seemed more than inviting.

Careful, she admonished herself as she again focused on her visitor's remarks.

"Your facility was recommended to me by my Denver surgeon. My left leg and hip were crushed in an automobile wreck six months ago." He fixed her with a keen, unwavering glance. "Perhaps you've heard about the accident?"

Connie thought for a moment. "Yes. I do remember the accident was reported on the evening television news."

"My wife was killed in the accident, and there was quite a lot of publicity."

What kind of publicity would cause his voice to tremble slightly when he mentioned it? she thought. Local accidents didn't usually cause a ripple in the news media unless the wreck was sensational, so what was unusual about the accident he mentioned?

"I'm sorry to hear about your loss."

"It's a miracle that I wasn't killed too, and considering the physical suffering of the past few months, there have been times when I wished I had died, but I'm still alive and disabled. The surgeons have done all they can and suggested that I enroll in a rehabilitation program."

"What do you know about our work here at NLC?" Connie asked, wondering if Joseph was the type to readily accept the strict regimen required at the Center.

"Not a thing," he said, and added with a broad smile, "I'd never heard of the place until yesterday. But what difference does it make? My surgeon said that you could recommend a physical program to strengthen my thigh and leg. What else do I need to know?"

"Quite a lot. You see, Mr. Caldwell, NLC's focus differs from most physical fitness centers. Our goal is to heal the mind and spirit as well as the body."

He laughed shortly. "There's nothing wrong with my mind and spirit. I have an injured limb. That's all I want from you."

Connie swiveled in her chair toward the cabinet behind her. She took out several pamphlets and handed them to Joseph, and when he refused to take them, she laid the booklets on the desk in front of him.

"I suggest you read those, Mr. Caldwell. You need to know the basic purpose of NLC before we can continue. I'll be in the office working with my secretary, and I'll talk with you again in a half hour."

Joseph's gray eyes hardened, and he glared at her. He hadn't picked up the brochures before she left the office and closed the door behind her. Kim turned questioning eyes in her direction, but Connie shrugged her shoulders and said, "Let's check through the bills we need to pay this month."

They'd been working about three minutes when her office door opened abruptly. A sardonic grin spreading across his face, Joseph ripped the pamphlets she'd given him and dropped the pieces into the wastepaper container.

"No, thanks, Miss Harmon. I won't accept your

services. I had enough Bible training when I was a child to do me a lifetime. I'll come here for physical training, but nothing else."

"You apparently didn't read enough to find out our application procedure, Mr. Caldwell. We have a limited clientele, and our staff decides who enrolls here. The patient doesn't have the last word."

Favoring his left leg, and leaning heavily on the cane, Joseph turned toward the door. "Then I'm sorry I bothered you, Miss Harmon."

Well, that takes care of rebounding into his arms! she thought.

Either from anger or fatigue, Joseph's body trembled as he walked down the hallway, and his leg buckled when he reached the foyer. If there hadn't been a couch handy, he'd have collapsed on the floor. Stifling a groan, he rubbed his thigh, which felt as if it was on fire. What was he going to do? Had he been too hasty in rejecting NLC's services? Joseph considered himself a man of integrity and truth, but he hadn't been completely honest with Connie Harmon. His life had been out of sync long before Virginia's death, and his injury and the unsettling incidents following the accident had shattered his peace of mind. Over the past six months, he didn't know which had been the most painful—his physical wounds or his mental anguish. Where had he gone wrong with Virginia? What had happened to the marriage that had started out so promising?

When the throbbing in his leg lessened to a dull ache, Joseph stood and started toward the door, but he sat down again. He remembered what Dr. Melrose had said the day before. "Joseph, I can't do anything more for you, but it *is* possible for you to be healed. You're fretting about the circumstances of Virginia's death, and that keeps you from concentrating on your recovery. Since you were driving, no doubt you feel guilty, and you'll have to move beyond that before you're physically well. I know a place that can help you.''

He'd spent many hours thinking about Dr. Melrose's recommendation, and he'd come to NLC this morning with a sense of anticipation. He was normally an even-tempered person, so why had he been so antagonistic toward Connie Harmon? Suddenly the answer was obvious. He'd experienced a physical attraction to her the minute she'd walked into the office, and he resented her because she'd sparked an emotional yearning he'd stifled for years. He had remained faithful to Virginia in spite of their problems, and after her death, he'd vowed to refrain from future involvement with women. Developing a romantic interest in Connie Harmon would be the worst thing that could happen to him now. Surely Dr. Melrose could recommend another facility that wasn't operated by a young, attractive woman who had shattered his determination to avoid the opposite sex with one lovely smile.

Joseph struggled to his feet again and started toward the door. He stopped and looked down the hallway. Was NLC his last hope for healing—and for living a normal life? If he left, would he always be physically handicapped? Did a new life await him if he stayed? He stood at the crossroads. Which way should he go?

As they listened to his faltering footsteps, Kim and

Connie exchanged glances. This wasn't the first irate prospect they'd lost, but Connie knew that Joseph desperately needed their services. Unless he recovered his mobility, his ability to operate his ranch would be limited.

"Too bad!" Kim said, her brown eyes wretched. "He's a man who needs some help."

"But he's apparently too proud to accept it. We can't help those who won't cooperate." Drawing a deep breath, Connie said, "I'm not in the mood for bills, but we might as well ruin the whole morning. Do we have the money to pay our debts?"

"Cheer up," Kim said, as she handed Connie a list of current expenditures and receipts. "We'll be a few dollars in the black this month."

Connie couldn't keep her mind on their work, and she finally leaned back in the chair. "I'd heard that Mr. Caldwell was injured in an auto accident that also resulted in the death of his wife. Do you know anything else about it?"

"Actually, I heard more about it than I wanted to," Kim said with a laugh. "When Virginia Caldwell was killed, Rose gave me a blow-by-blow description of everything that happened."

Surprised, Connie asked, "Rose Nash? Our cook?" Kim nodded.

"Why would she be interested?"

"She worked for Virginia Caldwell's family, the Perrys, for several years, when Virginia and her brother, George, were children. She was hired as the cook, but I've gathered she did some baby-sitting, too. The Perrys were rich socialites and they were away from home quite a lot. She also knew Joseph after he and Virginia were married.''

''I try not to listen to gossip,'' Connie said, ''but since I've heard this much, I might as well learn what else you know. I'm curious about him, and also interested in why his surgeon suggested NLC when there are so many excellent health centers in Denver. Does Joseph need more than physical therapy?''

''Virginia's death was caused by a blow to the head, but the authorities questioned whether she died from being struck during the accident, or from a fall she'd had earlier.''

''What do you mean?''

''According to Rose, Joseph found his wife unconscious and bleeding from a head wound, and he was taking her to the hospital when the accident occurred. There probably wouldn't have been an investigation, except for the note Virginia had sent to her brother the day before her death. I don't remember the exact words, but it was something like, 'He's got all of my money. I have nothing else to give him except my life. I'm afraid.' George Perry jumped to the conclusion that she meant Joseph and he went to the police.''

''I can't imagine how I missed all of that,'' Connie said.

''It could have been that time when we were short-handed. You were working long hours and didn't have the time to read the newspapers.''

''Have those suspicions been authenticated?''

''Rose hasn't mentioned it for several months, so I don't know anything more than that.''

They started checking the accounts again, and

they'd almost finished when a knock sounded on the door.

"Come in," Kim invited.

Joseph Caldwell stood diffidently in the open door. "I was a bit hasty in my departure, Miss Harmon. Perhaps we should have that talk."

Connie's pulse quickened. She would have been disappointed to have had no further contact with this man. "By all means. Come in the office. Don't interrupt me for phone calls, Kim."

She moved toward her office and Joseph followed. Watching the graceful sway of her shoulders, Joseph knew his decision to return had been influenced more by his desire to associate with NLC's proprietor than by the services the Center could provide. He could find another rehab facility, but where else would he find a woman whose presence gave him a reason, not only to recover physically, but perhaps even to live again? Momentarily, he was seized with the desire to hold Connie close and never let her go—a thought that amazed him so much that he stumbled and almost fell.

Connie turned immediately and grabbed his arm, a touch that electrified both of them, and for a moment, they stared incredulously into each other's eyes.

Connie released his arm, and striving to ignore the intimate moment they'd just experienced, Joseph carefully lowered his body into the chair and stretched out his leg.

"I apologize for my rudeness earlier," he said. "I'm not usually so short-tempered, but except for a few childhood illnesses I've never been sick, and for the past six months, I've been in and out of the hospital without gaining much help for my problem. That's caused me to become irritable.''

''I understand,'' she said.

''I'm only thirty-four years old, and it hurts my pride, as well as my hip, to move around like an old man. Dr. Melrose recommended you, saying you were my best chance for complete recovery.''

''I know Dr. Melrose well. He's sent several patients to us, including his own son. He was pleased with his son's progress.''

''I expected a conventional health center, not a religious spa,'' Joseph said bitterly. ''I don't have time to go to worship services every day. I've been away from my ranch off and on for months, and with summer coming, I need to be at home. How long do you think this will take?''

''I'm not a miracle worker, and if you expect me to use some mysterious hocus-pocus to bring about your healing, you may as well leave. God is important in the healing process, but it takes exercise, rest, proper diet, as well as spiritual commitment, to achieve a complete cure, and that takes time.''

''I've just explained to you that I don't have much time,'' he said tersely, then he laughed. ''We're going in circles, Miss Harmon. Someone has to budge, and since I'm the one asking for help, I guess I'll have to do it. What do you want me to do?''

''I'll take you on a tour of our facilities so you can see what we have to offer. Our physician will give you a brief exam, and you can fill out an application. We'll need a copy of your recent medical records, too. Our review board will study your case and decide if we can give you the help you need. If so, we'll assign a personal trainer to work with you and help implement a daily exercise program.''

"Do you know how long it will take?"

"Lacking any medical details of your injury, except what I've observed, I'd guess at least three months."

He shook his head and gritted his teeth, but he controlled his anger. "All summer!"

"We don't make prisoners of our therapy patients, but we do expect them to stay here five days a week, and they go home on weekends if they're able. Those who live at a distance often stay until their program is completed."

"My ranch is a hundred miles from here, and I'd have to go home periodically to oversee the work. My sister lives nearby and checks on the place every few days, but there are some decisions she can't make."

"Let's take a tour of the buildings now, and you can see what we have to offer. We have golf carts available for our patients to travel if they aren't able to walk. Are you up to walking?"

He grunted painfully as he got out of the chair. "I walk as much as possible, but I'm slow, and after a short time, I have to stop to rest."

"We can take all morning because I don't have an appointment until this afternoon. Let's go."

They went first to the gymnasium, located near the administration building. In general, Connie stayed away from the gym as much as possible to avoid Ray Blazer, the manager of the exercise rooms, but since she found it expedient to dispense with unpleasant encounters as quickly as possible, she started the tour there.

The gym provided the best exercise machines available. She and Joseph paused at the door of the fitness room to observe, and avoid the walkers who circled the indoor walking track, either cooling down after workouts, or getting their adrenaline pumping before strenuous exercise.

One elderly woman waved to Connie and rushed on. Amusement spread across Joseph's face as he observed the lady circling the track in a slow trot.

"Isn't she a little old for this activity?" he asked.

"Not at all. Della Sinnet is in her eighties, but she's a regular fixture around here," Connie said. "Her home is in Colorado Springs, but she spends her winters in a warmer climate. She comes to NLC for several weeks each spring, and she challenges all of us with her vitality."

"So you have patients of all ages," Joseph said as he observed the activities—people on treadmills, stationary bikes, stair-steppers, rowers and skate machines. In spite of the busyness, the atmosphere appeared calm, for quiet, classical, inspirational music wafted through the rooms. Videos provided soothing scenes of sunsets, towering trees, placid lakes, tranquil oceans and animals playing with their little ones. The room conveyed a pleasant feeling of exercising in the great outdoors.

Joseph followed Connie into the free-weight room where men and women worked on the equipment, seemingly without effort. "It'll be a long time before I'm ready for this equipment," he muttered.

"Not as long as you might think," Connie said.

She beckoned to a young man, who was coaching a woman on the horizontal calf raise machine. He ignored Connie for several minutes as he continued his instructions, then he sauntered toward them. Ray Blazer was a good advertisement for his profession. He had the build of a wrestler, and he kept in shape by exercising two hours each day on the free-weight machines.

"Mr. Caldwell, this is Ray Blazer, manager of the gym and an expert on physical fitness. He'll explain the various equipment to you. I'll be on a treadmill while Ray gives you a tour of our exercise facilities."

A patient stepped off a treadmill and moved to a modified leg stretch machine, so Connie got on the machine and adjusted it to her pace. She faced the weight room, so she'd know when Joseph was ready to leave. Ray moved from one machine to another explaining their various functions to Joseph.

Although Ray was an expert in his field, Connie wished he'd leave NLC. She'd been engaged to Ray until two months ago, and her disappointment in him still burned in her heart. When Ray came to the Center a year ago, it seemed the perfect situation—she could combine her work and romance. She'd thought she loved Ray, but when he disregarded her moral principles, which he'd known about before their engagement, she broke the engagement. But though she tried to avoid being alone with him, she couldn't drop him from her staff, and it presented a problem.

When Joseph limped in her direction, Connie stepped off the treadmill. "I must sit down," he muttered. "This leg gives me fits when I'm on it too long."

"That's understandable," Connie said. "Let's sit on the bench in front of the building, so we can enjoy the sunshine and fresh air." He held the door open for her, then he eased onto the bench with a deep sigh and closed his eyes.

Joseph breathed heavily, and pain etched deep lines on his face. Sitting beside him, their shoulders touching, Connie had the urge to run her fingers through his finely textured hair, and to wipe away the pain reflected on his face—an emotion that surprised her so much, she leaped to her feet and leaned against the building. When Joseph opened his eyes, he said, "I might as well go home, accept the fact that I'm handicapped, and learn to live with it. I'll never be able to manage those exercise machines."

"It's normal for you to feel like that. I pointed out Della Sinnet to you. She came to us using a walker soon after NLC opened. She'd had two hip replacements. None of us were optimistic about helping her, and there were days when she cried in frustration. After only a few minutes on the treadmill her body hurt so much she had to stop. But Della believed that 'with God, all things are possible,' and she kept at it. Slowly, we began to see progress, and the day that Della climbed Faith Mountain, we had a party."

"Faith Mountain? I've never heard of it."

Connie laughed. "Not many people have. It's a hill on our property, several hundred feet higher in altitude than we are here, but it's a steep climb to the top. When one of our patients is able to scale that hill, we know they've just about recovered."

"If an eighty-year-old can make it, perhaps I can,

too. I'm ready to continue the tour," Joseph said, struggling to his feet.

They checked out the pool area and the aerobic room, where exercises were in progress, before they reached the cafeteria.

"It's a little early, but let's have lunch anyway. You're our guest today, Joseph. Incidentally, we use first names at NLC."

"All health foods, I suppose," Joseph said, a twinkle in his gray eyes, as they entered a brightly decorated room that could seat fifty diners.

"All our meals are designed with health in mind, but we believe moderation is the key to good living, so the cooks provide occasional treats," Connie said as she directed Joseph to a small table beside a window. "There's a buffet in the evening, but we order from a menu for breakfast and lunch."

When they were seated, she took two menus from the rack and handed one to him. "Our sandwiches are served on whole wheat or rye bread, and everything is low-cal as much as possible. If you want a hot meal, I'd recommend the pasta dishes."

"Please order for me. I haven't paid much attention to my diet for several months. I don't care what I eat."

"Very well. We'll have the pasta and chicken, a vegetable salad with tarragon vinegar and a bowl of mixed fruit. Spring water for our beverage."

A waitress soon placed their meals before them, and Joseph attacked his food as if he hadn't eaten for a month, surprised that his appetite had returned. He couldn't remember when he'd been hungry. Appraising Connie obliquely, he wondered how much her presence contributed to his enjoyment of the meal.

Questioning what had happened to her appetite, Connie picked at her pasta. Habitually, she never left a morsel of food on her plate, but Joseph's keen, appraising glances unnerved her. Remembering that electric moment in the office, she wondered if he sensed the attraction between them also. Finally, she pushed the pasta and salad aside and nibbled on the mixed fruit.

When the silence became unbearable, she directed the conversation to Joseph's ranch, and they talked amicably while they ate.

"I went to college, intending to study ophthalmology, but, after a year, I knew I couldn't spend my life tied to an office. Ranching was what I loved, so I changed my major to agriculture, which pleased my father. He was nearing retirement age, and he wanted me to take over the ranch."

As Joseph described the changes he'd made at the ranch since his father's retirement, he seemed to forget his physical and emotional problems. They'd just finished eating when the kitchen door opened and a plump, graying woman in her fifties approached their table.

Remembering what Kim had told her, Connie hoped this encounter wouldn't embarrass Joseph, but when Rose stopped beside them, Connie said, "Mr. Caldwell, this is our head cook, Rose Nash—the one responsible for the good meal we've enjoyed. Rose, this is Joseph Caldwell. He's looking over our facility today."

"Oh, I know Mr. Caldwell," she said.

Joseph looked up quickly, and rose awkwardly to his feet. His face registered astonishment, but not guilt or displeasure, as he shook Rose's hand.

"This is a surprise, Rose! I didn't know what happened to you after Mr. Perry died. I'm glad to see you. You're looking—" he hesitated "—fit."

Rose threw back her head and laughed heartily. "Don't you mean *fat?* I try to eat the food Connie prescribes, but I'd overindulged too long before I came to NLC. She hasn't given up on me yet—I've only been here a year."

"Sit down, Rose," Connie invited. "You probably need a break."

Rose took the chair between them, explaining, "Connie, I was employed by Mr. Caldwell's in-laws for several years."

"And I remember all the good food you served us," Joseph said.

"Like that chocolate-pecan pie you liked so well?" Favoring Connie with a mischievous glance, Rose said, "I brought a big box of recipes from the Perry home. If I can find the directions for that pie, I'll bake one for you."

"That will definitely be a factor in my decision. I'll keep it in mind."

Connie listened silently while Joseph and Rose talked about the Perrys, and the childhood of Virginia and George, her brother. The conversation was lighthearted until Rose stood up. "Time for me to go back to work. It's almost noon, and I'll be busy. It's good to see you again, Mr. Caldwell. I'm sorry you and George are having problems—you were always such good buddies."

A somber expression clouded Joseph's face, and he said stiffly, "I'm sorry, too, but I suppose he's doing what he thinks is right."

Leaving the dining room, Connie noticed that Joseph walked with increasing difficulty, and she pointed to a golf cart parked nearby. "Let's take the rest of the tour on wheels, for I have an appointment in about an hour."

She wanted to save his pride by suggesting the cart was for her benefit, but when he put his arm on her shoulder for added support as he eased into the seat, a little twinge of excitement flowed into her heart. It's high time you get your emotions under control, she admonished herself sternly. But she wasn't sure her heart received the message.

Chapter Two

NLC was located on a thirty-acre tract of land in a remote valley. The facility had been built for a convention center, but when the firm that owned the center failed, Connie bought the place. What had once been a forty-room motel turned into a dormitory for residents. If they preferred, patients could lodge in one of ten two-room rustic cabins. NLC had a well-equipped kitchen and spacious dining area, and an inside Olympic-size pool with sliding doors, which opened during the warm season to give the illusion of outdoor bathing.

Connie drove past the small chapel, the dormitory, the shaded area by the creek where the log cabins were located and along a few of the walking trails.

Returning to the administration building, she said, "Our physician has his offices here, and he's on campus two days each week. You'll need to see him for a brief exam. He checks each of our patients weekly, so he's busy, but I think he'll be available today."

"What's my next move? When will you tell me if I've been accepted?"

"Our advisory board meets tomorrow evening, so if you'll come back or telephone midmorning two days from now, I'll give you an answer. A client is assigned to a personal trainer, chosen according to the workload of the employee. If the trainer and patient aren't compatible, we make another assignment."

Connie accompanied Joseph to the reception room of Dr. Ron Alexander. Peggy McCane, the nurse, said the doctor could see him within the hour. Tall, lanky Peggy had been at the Center for over a year, and she was Connie's jogging partner. Since her broken engagement two months ago, Connie no longer ran alone.

"I'll leave you now, Joseph. You're in good hands with Peggy and Dr. Alexander."

Joseph shifted his cane to his left hand and shook hands with her. Candidly, he said, "I should warn you, Miss Harmon, I'm a cantankerous patient—you may want to take that into consideration during your staff conference."

She returned his grasp, noting that his fingers were strong and capable, but quickly disengaged her hand, unprepared for the tingling sensation triggered by his touch. The more difficult Joseph was, the less likely she would be to succumb to his charm. If he compelled her admiration when he winced with pain at every step, she couldn't imagine how attractive she'd find him when he was physically fit. When she'd once watched his rodeo exhibition, Connie had been impressed with the suppleness and grace of his body, and she'd never forgotten his superb performance.

Yes, it would definitely be more beneficial to her peace of mind if Joseph was a disagreeable patient.

"That won't make any difference. We don't shy away from difficult cases—they present a challenge. We're dedicated to meeting the needs of our patients at their level. Bye."

With a wave of her hand, Connie sprinted down the hall to her office. She was next in line on the staff to take a new patient. Should she decline to work with Joseph? She had no doubt that he would demand all of her therapy skills before he achieved complete mobility, but that didn't worry her. She'd never doubted her skill as a therapist, yet she did question her ability to deal with Joseph without becoming personally involved with him. She'd had no trouble in the past staying on an impersonal level with her patients. Would working with Joseph challenge her self-control?

After Joseph left the doctor's office, he got into his pickup to return to the ranch. His troubled mind superceded his eagerness to get home, so instead of heading toward the interstate and a quick trip to the ranch, he turned northward on a narrow, winding road through the mountains. After several miles, he stopped at an observation point that provided an unobstructed view of Long's Peak.

The encounter with Rose Nash had flooded his mind with memories that he wanted to forget. In spite of the suspicions of his brother-in-law and the police, he hadn't killed Virginia, but had his actions driven his wife to her death? If he could rid himself of the guilty feeling that he'd indirectly caused her to die, he thought he could regain his physical health.

He'd fallen in love with Virginia at their first meeting. Their whirlwind courtship had soon led to a proposal, and he couldn't believe his good fortune when she'd wanted to marry him.

They'd been deliriously happy for the first year, but Joseph had become disillusioned when he'd realized they had very little in common. His wife had detested his rural lifestyle, while he'd resented the money showered on Virginia by her parents—money that enabled her to spend winter months in Florida or California with the friends she'd had before they were married.

Joseph wasn't good at pretense, and when his love dwindled, he could no longer treat Virginia with the affection she craved. When she'd wandered away, he'd done nothing to prevent it.

When his love for Virginia had been at its peak, he realized that his regard for God had sunk to its lowest ebb, and when he'd no longer loved her, he was still out of fellowship with God. Once the close relationship with his wife and with God was gone, he didn't know how to regain either of them.

Joseph stepped out of the truck, and leaned against the stone barrier at the edge of the precipice. From his pocket, he took out a New Testament that a chaplain at the hospital had given him. When Joseph had complained that God seemed so far away, the chaplain had answered, "God hasn't moved—you have," and he'd quoted a verse from the writings of Solomon. "'I know that everything God does will endure forever.' Once you've trusted God for your daily provision and your eternal salvation, it's a done deal. Your affections may wane, but God is always there—faithful and steadfast.''

Joseph turned to a Psalm that had once been meaningful to him. "Whom have I in heaven but You? And being with You, I desire nothing on earth."

He bowed his head and longed for the day when he could regain the fellowship he'd once had with God.

The advisory board met the next night to consider several applicants. Files on each of them had been provided to board members in advance. Kim attended the meetings, not only as a voting member, but to keep records of the proceedings. They met in the reception room beside Connie's office. Chaplain Eric Sadler, Dr. Alexander, Ray Blazer, Connie and Kim were permanent members of the board. Other staff members came periodically to report on the progress of their patients. Four out of five of the permanent members had to agree on applicants before they were accepted. Ever since Connie had broken her engagement to Ray, he was often obstinate during this decision making, especially if he thought Connie was particularly keen on accepting the individual.

Ray opposed Joseph's application immediately. "The man is suspected of murdering his wife. His presence would be bad publicity for NLC."

"If he's in trouble, he probably needs our ministry more than many others," Connie replied evenly.

"It's my opinion," Eric stated, "that the larger the problem, the greater our responsibility to deal with it. If Mr. Caldwell is innocent, he must be carrying a heavy emotional burden, in addition to his physical problems.''

Dr. Alexander, a middle-aged, tall, heavyset bachelor, nodded agreement. ''I haven't received his records yet, but I did talk to his surgeon, Dr. Melrose. He concludes that Mr. Caldwell's mental anguish is partly responsible for the slow healing of his body, and that's why he recommended NLC as the place for him. Dr. Melrose also believes in Caldwell's innocence. I'm in favor of accepting his application.''

Joseph was accepted by a vote of four to one, with Ray dissenting. Connie was assigned to be his personal trainer.

When the meeting adjourned, Ray fell in step with Connie as she walked down the hallway. ''I want to talk to you, Connie.''

''Go ahead,'' she said.

''Not here. Let's take a drive.''

She shook her head. ''No, Ray.''

''Don't you trust me?''

''How could I? But in any case we have nothing to say to each other.''

''Don't you trust yourself? By refusing to be alone with me, are you afraid I'll break down your feeble defenses?''

Connie didn't answer, but continued doggedly toward the dormitory, and the small apartment on the first floor that she shared with Kim. Considering the growing relationship between Kim and Eric, the chaplain, Connie knew she might soon be staying in the apartment alone.

''Let me come in for a few minutes. You can't be serious about breaking our engagement. You've had time to think about this. Everybody deserves a second chance."

He followed her into the foyer, and Connie motioned to a couch near the door.

"I don't have anything to say, Ray, but if you'll be brief, I'll listen," she said curtly.

When they were seated, he took her hand. "If you won't agree to live with me for a year's trial, we'll go ahead and get married now." From his pocket, he withdrew the diamond solitaire she'd returned, and when he tried to put it on her finger, she shoved his hand away.

"You still don't agree with my conviction that couples should avoid intimacy until after marriage. Since I'm the coordinator of the local Marriage First support group, I won't have a spouse who opposes that concept."

Connie fingered the pin on the lapel of her blouse. In a gold setting, a pair of intertwined wedding bands and the slogan, Marriage First, stated the group's purpose. In an age when the institution of marriage was being threatened by divorce and premarital sex, Connie and her friends had joined other groups nationwide to encourage abstinence. Ray had laughed at her beliefs, and she found that hard to forgive.

"But you still want me," Ray said, and he bent forward to kiss her. Connie moved to elude his gesture.

"No, that isn't true. I was unhappy at first, and disillusioned, but I've gotten over it, and I don't want to renew our relationship."

"But you will think about it?" Ray insisted.

Connie agreed, adding, "But I don't expect to

change. I'm happy with things the way they are now.''

Ray stomped toward the open door and out into the night. He lived in one of the two-room cabins, and Connie supposed he was going there, but she heard his Jeep's motor start, and he drove by at a reckless speed, apparently heading for town. Had she been wrong to turn him down? Did he deserve a second chance?

She was startled out of her reverie by Della, who was coming down the hall swathed in a terry cloth robe, with a towel thrown over her shoulder.

''I'm going for a swim. The pool will be open for another hour. Why don't you come with me?''

Connie jumped up from the couch. ''Just what I need! Give me a few minutes to change, and I'll join you.'' Della was doing push-ups when Connie came back into the foyer. ''Don't you ever run out of energy?'' Connie said, laughing. ''At this time of day, I hardly have enough steam to take a few laps across the pool.''

Della bounded to her feet. ''That's because you're not old enough. It takes years to build up enough stamina to get over the hump.''

''Do you expect to live forever?'' Connie joked.

''Nope, but I want to feel good as long as I'm here. I aim to leave earth with a shout and head upward like Elijah did. I don't intend to cripple into heaven.''

Della hooked her arm into Connie's as they left the dorm. ''Excuse me for eavesdropping, but I was coming down the hall and heard your conversation with Ray. I waited until you'd finished, not wanting to interrupt.''

"Did I do the right thing, Della? Should I marry him?"

"That's a question I can't answer for you, honey." Everybody was "honey" to Della, who humorously admitted that she called everyone that because her memory was so faulty she couldn't remember names.

"I know I'm the only one who can make that decision. When I agreed to marry Ray, I thought that was the right decision. And when I broke our engagement, I felt that was right, too. I don't want to make another mistake."

"I'm not sure either of those decisions were mistakes. How would you have known the depth of your commitment to the Marriage First ideal unless you were tested? But you may be facing your toughest choice now—whether or not to take Ray back."

"I thought marriage to Ray would be perfect. We were both dedicated to physical fitness, and I believed we could become partners here at NLC, as well as in marriage."

"Honey, no marriage is perfect. It takes work from both parties to even have a good marriage, and there isn't any perfection this side of heaven. But, besides your profession, what else did you and Ray have in common?"

"Not much," Connie admitted ruefully, "and that should have been a warning for me. Since childhood my parents have quoted the Scripture to me, 'Do not be yoked together with unbelievers. For what do righteousness and wickedness have in common?' They weren't pleased with my choice of Ray, but I thought I knew more than my parents."

"I've noticed Ray's scornful expression in morning

worship, and I question that he believes a word of Eric's messages. You need to consider the depth of his spiritual life in making a decision.''

''The way I feel now, remembering how angry and forceful he became, I'll never marry him. I hoped we could remain friends as long as he works here, but I'm starting to doubt that. I'm afraid of Ray, and that keeps me uneasy.''

''I pray you'll find the right mate, honey. I've buried two husbands, and I loved both of them. I can't imagine what it would be like to be married to someone you couldn't respect, and I hope you never find out. Keep yourself pure until you find the man who shares your ideals.''

''I intend to, but I sometimes wonder if there is a man like that.''

''There are lots of them, honey. Don't let Ray pressure you—wait until you're sure.''

The pool wasn't crowded, so Connie pulled off her robe and eased into the tepid water. She paused to admire the skill of Bobby Richie, a young athlete who was a regular in NLC's weight room during football season. This summer, he'd signed up for NLC's body building program in preparation for a cross-country bicycle trek. He sprang from the board, executed a graceful somersault and dived into the water.

After swimming the length of the pool six times, Connie felt refreshed and glad she'd come, for the tension she'd experienced during the meeting—and while she'd talked with Ray—had eased. She'd once looked forward to their weekly board meetings, but she didn't any longer. She was always edgy, wondering what Ray would do next. Why was Ray biased against Joseph?

Connie waved to Della, who rested on the side of the pool, waiting to plunge into the water again. On the way back to her apartment, Connie turned aside to the chapel and sat in the back pew. Connie's father, a machinery salesman, had located the abandoned pioneer log church in the western part of the state, and her parents had helped her dismantle the building, log by log, and arrange to have it hauled to the Center, where Connie had hired a builder to reassemble the chapel.

Each morning when Eric conducted the half hour service, he stood behind a hand-carved lectern that she'd found in an antique shop and had painstakingly restored to its original splendor. A small electronic organ was used for congregational singing, but the remainder of the time, quiet, taped music lent an atmosphere of peace and hope to the small room. A few minutes of meditation in the chapel always lifted Connie's spirits as she looked at a large painting behind the pulpit depicting Christ's healing of the crippled man at the pool of Bethesda.

In the early days, when she'd had so much trouble getting the Center started, and when financial straits made her wonder if the work was worthwhile, Connie had often come to the chapel and focused her attention on Jesus and the man He'd healed, which reminded her of the first line of a poem she'd once read—when the author had suggested that Christ used the hands of others to do His work. When Jesus went back to Heaven after His years on earth, He'd commissioned His followers to continue His mission. Connie considered herself in partnership with Jesus to bring hope to the disabled as He had done.

Joseph Caldwell came to mind. She welcomed the challenge to work with him until he could walk with the assurance and the erect bearing he'd possessed when she'd seen him on television. Thinking of him made her wonder about Ray's antipathy toward Joseph. She supposed she was foolish, but she suspected that Ray didn't want her in Joseph's company, as if he were jealous of him. She'd shown no more interest in Joseph than she had any other potential patient of NLC. Or had she? Had she inadvertently revealed her uncommon interest in Joseph and his affairs? She must exercise more self-control where he was concerned.

Or did Ray know something about Joseph that she should know? If she'd learned anything from her disappointing relationship with Ray, it was to steer clear of anyone who didn't share her Christian beliefs. And she was pretty sure that Joseph didn't. She'd been burned once—that should've taught her to stay away from the fire. Her face flushed when she thought of working with Joseph. She'd almost refused to be his personal trainer, for his was the only assignment she'd ever taken in which she thought of her client more as a *man* rather than a *patient.* If she felt that way about him now, what would happen when she spent time with him every day for three months? Just thinking about their hours of togetherness left her breathless.

But she hadn't come here to think about Joseph. Ray was her main concern now. Did she love him? At one time, she'd had no doubt. Did her love die, or had she ever truly loved him? Connie had no desire to marry Ray now. She couldn't imagine spending the rest of her life with a man who used force to achieve his objectives. But should he continue in the employ of NLC? Ray was an expert in his field, and he would be hard to replace.

When she left the chapel, Connie hadn't gotten the answers she'd come to find.

Connie awoke to bright sunshine and the sound of a white-winged dove cooing outside her window. She threw back the covers and hit the floor with a song bursting from her lips. She couldn't match the dove's refrain, but she had a melody of her own.

Kim's bed was neatly made, and the apartment was empty. Kim had already gone for her early-morning swim.

Changing into sweats, and feeling a tremendous joy in the new day, Connie joined Peggy on the two-mile round-trip run they took every morning. Joseph would be coming to the Center today, and she fleetingly wondered if that was the reason for her joyful attitude. Of course it was, for she always looked forward to helping a new patient—her excitement didn't have anything to do with the captivating masculinity that, in spite of his disability, Joseph radiated.

Connie waited in her office, and when Joseph didn't telephone, she wondered if he'd decided not to come, but she soon heard his halting tread in the corridor. Kim greeted him warmly, and said, "Connie is in her office. Go on in."

Joseph paused with his hand on the doorknob, feeling giddy at the thought of seeing Connie again.

She'd been uppermost in his thoughts for two days, and he blushed when he remembered that her presence had even infiltrated his dreams. Banishing such thoughts from his mind, he entered the room and closed the door behind him.

Joseph was dressed in jeans and a red-plaid flannel shirt that lent color to his face, which had grown pale during his hospital confinement. During previous television interviews, Joseph had always appeared as a tanned and hardy outdoorsman, and his casual appearance today pleased Connie.

After they were seated, he said, with some apprehension and a hint of belligerence, "Well, was I accepted or not?"

"Yes. We're willing to give it a try if you are."

"The sooner the better," he muttered. "My leg has been giving me fits this morning. I brought my luggage."

With a gleam in her eyes, she said, "You were unfortunate enough to draw me for your personal trainer. We rotate assignments based on workload, and since we discharged one of my patients last week, I was next in line for an assignment. After a week, if we aren't compatible, you can have another trainer."

"Why wouldn't we be?"

Considering her sensitivity to Joseph's physical appeal, Connie knew very well why it might be necessary to appoint a different trainer for him, but she said evenly, "It doesn't happen often, but we've had a few cases of personality conflicts, and when that happens, the patient is given the option to have another trainer."

"I'm sure we'll get along all right," Joseph said

with a grin. "I'm peaceable until the pain gets too bad."

Connie picked up a folder from her desk. "Let's sit at the conference table," she said, indicating an oval table near the window. Joseph pulled out a chair, seated Connie, then took the chair beside her. She spread out several sheets of paper.

"I've planned a three-month program for you."

"You still think it will take that long?"

"Probably. We'll start slowly and gradually work up to your potential. I want you to walk out of here at the end of three months as physically fit as you were when I saw you ride a bucking bronco at the state fair two years ago."

"You saw that, did you?" His gray eyes flashed with pleasure.

"On television—but it impressed me."

"Bronc riding is a hobby for me, and most of my riding has been local. I thought my rodeo days were over, but I'm beginning to hope again. Dr. Melrose said that NLC would have that effect on me."

"We'll make every effort. Today, we'll settle you into a dorm room and do a few exercises." She handed him several sheets of paper. "Tomorrow, we'll start on this schedule, and then add a little more distance and additional exercises each day."

He glanced through the papers. "Looks as if I'll be busy enough."

"Our residents work at their own speed. Some are up at the break of dawn, swimming, jogging or working out in the gym. The day's schedule for everyone begins with worship services at half-past seven, and breakfast at eight. I always go jogging and shower before chapel, but until you're stronger, you should wait until after breakfast to start your physical activity. Other meals are at noon and six o'clock in the evening. Three meals a day and chapel are mandatory. Otherwise, it's up to the trainer and the client to decide on the individual's program."

"Do you actually believe that Christian worship makes a difference in the healing process?"

"Absolutely! It's been proven that people with a strong, practicing faith heal faster than those who don't believe in God."

"I've read those reports, but the people who heal more rapidly are those suffering from depression, hypertension, heart disease and similar problems—not anyone with an injury like mine."

"You're right to a degree, but one medical school study found that deeply religious surgical patients are less likely to die than those who find no comfort in religion."

"I don't believe it, but at this point, I'm desperate enough to try anything. I'll attend chapel."

"Even if you don't achieve complete healing, if your spirit is freed, you won't mind the physical injury so much."

Connie didn't think she'd convinced him, but Joseph glanced through the papers. "So my goal for the first week is to walk a mile and back, starting at nine o'clock each morning."

"Yes. The first days, you won't be able to walk that far, but hopefully you'll be able to by the end of the week. After the walk, you should rest in your room, and then spend an hour in the pool before lunch. In the afternoon, you can work in the gym at your own speed.''

''I notice you don't have anything scheduled for evenings. Is that time reserved so the patient can take his trainer out for dinner?'' Joseph hoped his expression didn't reveal his consternation. What had prompted him to make such a suggestion?

Startled, Connie swung a quick look in his direction, and their gazes locked for a few tense seconds. Connie deliberately ignored his remark and stacked the papers in front of her in an effort to regain her composure.

''A masseur and a masseuse come from Denver each evening, and many clients find it beneficial to have a massage several times a week. There are support group sessions where patients talk over the problems they're having. We show movies each night— nothing but comedies because laughter, too, is a part of the healing process. Or evening can be a good time to enjoy the peace and solitude of our surroundings. I'm proud of the grounds here at NLC—they're especially lovely in the spring.''

''The lake near the gate is beautiful,'' Joseph drawled, chastened by her silent reprimand. Well, he'd asked for it. His remark was out of line.

''There are benches around the lake,'' Connie continued, and he couldn't tell from her voice if she was annoyed with him, ''and many of our clients find it restful to sit and watch the ducks. The lake is stocked with fish, too, if you're interested in fishing.''

''I've done a lot of trout fishing, but I prefer to do that in a mountain current.'' His face hardened and his gray eyes dulled, and Connie suspected Joseph wondered how he could ever stand again in a cold mountain stream when he couldn't even walk unaided.

Connie joined Joseph in his blue pickup, and they drove to the dorm. "I arranged for you to sleep on the second floor because climbing stairs will be beneficial to you. However, there's an elevator to use when necessary. You must *not* overtax your strength! Most clients push themselves too much at first and become discouraged when they don't see immediate results. In fact, strenuous exercise at first does more harm than good."

The gardener was working in the flower beds in front of the dorm building, and he took the luggage upstairs by the elevator. Connie wanted to see Joseph's performance on the stairs, but seeing the way he winced on each step, she wished she hadn't asked him to try.

Joseph sat down immediately when they reached his room, and although his breath came in uneven gasps, he complimented Connie on the accommodations. The rooms varied in size, but she'd arranged for Joseph to have a large one with a king-size bed and a view of the mountains. A Bible on the night table lay open to a highlighted verse in the book of Isaiah. "Even youths grow tired and weary, and young men stumble and fall; but those who hope in the Lord will renew their strength. They will soar on wings like eagles; they will run and not grow weary, they will walk and not be faint."

Paintings by local artists decorated the walls, and a large cross-stitched sampler facing the bed was embroidered with a Bible verse from I Corinthians.

"Your body is a temple of the Holy Spirit, who is in you, whom you have received from God. You are not your own; you were bought at a price. Therefore, honor God with your body."

Joseph glanced out the window. "This is a peaceful setting," he said. "The large kitchen window in my house faces the mountains, too. It used to be a peaceful place."

Did the death of his wife keep him from finding any pleasure in his home? It shouldn't be surprising that Joseph would be depressed over the tragic events in his life during the past year. Had it been a happy marriage?

"What's on the program for this afternoon?"

Connie had intended for him to take a short walk, but suddenly she was overwhelmed with the desire to know more about Joseph—not just as a patient of NLC, but as a person. Besides, she thought climbing the stairs had overtaxed his strength.

"Tomorrow morning will be soon enough to start your exercises, so I propose we go on a picnic to Paddy's Point, NLC's most scenic spot, this afternoon. It's located along a graveled road that leads to our reservoir, and we can travel on the Center's ATV. Or would you prefer to rest?"

"Not at all. I haven't been on a picnic for years."

"On second thought—with your injury, the ATV may be too rough for you."

He grinned. "Not as long as you drive."

"Take a half hour to rest, and I'll check with Rose about our food."

After Connie left, Joseph stretched out on the bed, but he didn't sleep. Would his awareness of Connie as a desirable young woman interfere with his therapy sessions? He'd married Virginia for "better or worse," and even when their marriage soured, his thoughts and actions had remained faithful. He didn't take any pride in his restraint, for he hadn't seen another woman who'd interested him until he met Connie.

Virginia had frequent mood swings. For months she might be sweet, vibrant, attentive, then suddenly she would become depressed and uncommunicative. Upon her parents' insistence, she'd once been tested for being manic-depressive, but when the tests had proven negative, she'd discontinued her medication. His quiet wife had been a sharp contrast to Connie's outgoing, vibrant personality, and he wondered if he'd have the strength to resist her when he was in her presence for three months. He had enough trouble without developing a romantic bent for Connie.

As long as suspicion of Virginia's death shadowed him, he had to focus on his legal situation. When he regained his mobility, Joseph was determined to find out what had really happened in the days and weeks prior to his wife's death. He remembered a Bible verse he'd learned as a youth. "The truth will set you free." He'd never be free until he learned the truth about Virginia's death.

Chapter Three

Wondering what had possessed her to make such a suggestion, Connie hurried toward the cafeteria. She'd never picnicked alone with another patient!

"Hi, Rose," she called as she entered the kitchen. "Could you pack a lunch for me? Mr. Caldwell isn't ready for exercise this afternoon, and I suggested taking him on a picnic at Paddy's Point."

Connie fidgeted while Rose rummaged in the cabinets and refrigerator. Was it too late to change her mind? Or did she have a mind where Joseph was concerned? Joseph was like no man she'd ever known, and her behavior was worse than a girl with her first teenage crush.

"Here you are," Rose said, approaching with a small basket. "Cold grilled chicken breasts, tomatoes, apples, bread, yogurt and iced tea. Anything else?"

"No, that's fine. I didn't expect a feast on such an impromptu request."

Connie hurried away before Rose could ask any

questions. The ATV hadn't been used for a couple of weeks, but the motor started on the first try, and Connie drove it out of the garage and stopped in front of the dorm. She fastened the basket on the rear of the vehicle.

Connie hurriedly went to the apartment to change into jeans, and Joseph was waiting by the vehicle when she returned.

"Are you sure you don't want to drive?" she asked. "I've only operated this thing a few times."

He shook his head. "We have an ATV at the ranch, and I can give you advice if you need it. I don't want to risk hurting my leg by driving, but a four-wheeler isn't much rougher than a truck. Drive slowly, and there won't be any problem."

Still with some hesitation, she held Joseph's arm while he carefully and slowly lifted his left leg over the driver's seat, perched over the rear wheels of the ATV, and stretched out his injured limb. Once he was settled, Connie sat on the padded seat behind the wheel. Joseph hardly knew what to do with his hands, but Connie said, "Put your arms around my waist. I'll try to drive carefully, but you need to be able to steady yourself."

Joseph did as she said, but not without misgiving. Had he suffered a momentary mental relapse to agree to this strenuous excursion? And what about the injury to his heart—a heart already bruised and vulnerable? But he gritted his teeth, determined to endure with composure any pain to his injured hip or any emotional stress incurred from physical nearness to Connie.

When she'd always advised her staff to avoid personal encounters with their patients, Connie was hard put to understand why she'd suggested this outing with Joseph. There wasn't anything she could do now, but she vowed that this was just a one-time incident. Regardless of today's outcome, she would know better in the future. With these thoughts, she salved her conscience as, mindful of Joseph's injury, she put the vehicle slowly into motion. But her conscience didn't have to deal, as Connie did, with Joseph's soft breath on her neck, the firmness of his arms around her waist, nor the strength of his hands clasped in front of her.

Joseph needed NLC, but Connie didn't need the frustrations his presence provoked, and she wondered how she could endure three months of daily interaction with him and retain a strict patient-therapist relationship. Did she have the strength to remain dispassionate to this man who'd captivated her thoughts since the first day she'd met him?

When they entered the forest behind the chapel, the trail curved steadily upward. Connie shifted into a lower gear and glanced over her shoulder.

"Okay?"

"Not a twinge so far. You're a careful driver."

"Paddy's Point is only two miles on this trail, but it's too far for you to walk," she shouted, as she revved the motor and moved forward. The vehicle lurched into a small ditch, and Joseph's chin bumped into Connie's head.

"Sorry," he said.

"Did that jolt your leg?" she yelled, for the noise of the engine was deafening.

"Don't worry about me—I'm fine."

They soon arrived at a scenic spot, where a few years earlier, a forest fire had destroyed the tall trees, making way for a new stand of aspens and pines. Several miles to the west, the mountains around Berthoud Pass lifted their majestic peaks skyward. A small table and two benches provided a resting place for patients who jogged along this path. They were hailed by a couple of teenagers from Lakewood, who came to NLC daily to work out in the gym and test their endurance by climbing Faith Mountain and jogging back on the reservoir trail.

Joseph grunted as he laboriously raised his injured limb and eased off the four-wheeler. Connie stood by, ready to assist him if necessary. Joseph gasped, grabbed his cane for support, and stood for a few minutes before he limped to the table and sat heavily on the bench facing westward. When Connie brought the food basket, his eyes were fixed on the distant mountains, but noting the bleakness expressed on his face, she surmised he wasn't observing the beauty of nature.

"It's hard for me not to be angry when I see those two kids running down a trail like that, when I can't even walk."

Ever conscious of the purpose of NLC—to heal the body *and* the spirit—Connie pondered her reply as she spread a cloth on the table and set out the food items Rose had packed for them.

"Was the accident your fault?" she asked.

"Of course not," he said indignantly. "I was taking my wife to the hospital, and we were traveling in a blizzard, with visibility at zero level. A truck came around a curve in the road, skidded, and we hit head-on.''

"Then, why are you carrying around a load of guilt?''

"Hey,'' Joseph said angrily. "Are you a psychiatrist? My mind doesn't need to be healed. I don't want you probing around.''

"I've had a lot of psychology training, and I told you the first day that we work with the spirit as well as the body. It's a two-fold program. I'm not interested in your past,'' and as Connie said the words, she doubted she was being completely truthful, "but you strike me as a man who has a load of worry on his mind. Even Dr. Melrose's report indicated as much, but he wasn't specific.''

He didn't answer, and Connie said, "When you're ready to talk, I'm ready to listen, but let's have our picnic and enjoy the beauty of God's creation. Tomorrow, you start the hard stuff, so you need relaxation today.''

Ignoring his silence, Connie offered a brief prayer of thanks for the food. On a paper plate, she laid a piece of chicken, a slice of bread, quartered one of the tomatoes and placed it in front of him.

"I hope you like iced tea—that's all I have except water.''

He nodded, his face still gloomy. She placed the plate and beverage in front of him.

He sipped the tea. "No sugar?'' Joseph asked grumpily.

Biting her lip to keep from laughing, Connie reached in the basket. "One or two packets?''

With a sheepish grin, he said, "I don't want any

sugar. I'm wallowing in self-pity, and I was ready to be angry if you told me I couldn't have any sugar.''

Connie's laugh bubbled. ''You told me you'd be cantankerous, but I didn't expect you to be childish.''

He laughed lowly, and Connie was glad he hadn't taken offense at her words. ''You might as well learn the worst about me as soon as possible. Sit down and eat your lunch. You don't have to wait on me. I've prepared more than one meal for myself.''

Connie sat beside Joseph, and made a sandwich of the chicken and bread.

Still moody, Joseph said, ''I don't suppose you know what's it's like to have your life put on hold— everything you want to do pushed on the back burner—your whole life disrupted in a matter of seconds.''

Connie nibbled on a tomato wedge before she said, ''As a matter of fact, I do, but I don't want to talk about that now.''

''So you understand why I didn't want to talk about the accident—it's still too painful.''

''Certainly, I understand. I'm not pushing you.''

Except for an occasional comment about the food, they ate in silence until their initial hunger was sated. The serenity and the beauty of the spot soothed Joseph. His leg pained him, and he dreaded climbing back on the ATV for the downhill ride, but except for that, he was comfortable with Connie. He experienced peace and contentment he hadn't known in years. How much should he tell her? Or should he tell her anything?

''I won't talk about the time my future plans were disrupted,'' Connie said, disturbing his thoughts, ''but

I do understand how frustrating a physical disability can be. I know from experience how difficult it is to be unable to walk properly.''

He turned to stare at her, his gray eyes incredulous. "I can't believe you've ever been sick a day in your life."

"Oh, but I have. When I was born, my left leg was shorter than the other, and I limped badly when I started walking. My parents were afraid I'd always be crippled, but they were people of prayer, and they made up their minds that they wouldn't accept my disability as permanent. So they prayed for my healing, and asked others to pray, and I sincerely believe that the reason I'm walking normally today is due to Divine healing. I went through a rough childhood at fitness centers, taking stretching exercises and strengthening my body in general."

Joseph's expression softened to hope. "And that's all it took?"

"Not exactly. They kept me on a strict diet so I wouldn't gain weight, and gradually my leg lengthened. One day, when I was ten years old, I was reading the Bible incident about Jesus healing a man's arm, and I actually felt my leg stretch until it was the same length as the other one."

Joseph's face registered skepticism as she talked, so she was surprised at his next comment.

"He said to the man, 'Stretch out your hand.' He stretched it out, and his hand was completely restored."

Connie's eyebrows lifted. "So you *are* familiar with the Bible!"

"When I was a child, my parents forced me to

spend every Sunday afternoon memorizing Bible verses, and that was enough Scripture to last a lifetime. I haven't read the Bible since I left home.''

Considering his attitude, Connie wondered how she could encourage spiritual and physical healing in a man who had so definitely turned away from God's word.

''You were completely healed?'' Joseph asked.

''Yes, but the left leg isn't as strong as the other one, so I've continued my exercise program. God did his part, and I do mine.''

''And that's why you became a physical therapist?''

She nodded. ''I'd been in and out of gyms most of my life, learning the importance of maintaining a strong, healthy body. When it was time for me to decide on a career, I remembered the story of the four men who brought their friend to Jesus for healing. Jesus forgave the man's sins before He cured his disability, saying He healed the man when He saw the faith of his friends. I believe spiritual commitment has a great deal to do with the health of the body, and that God enables His followers to bring about that healing.''

Joseph removed the cover and took several bites of the strawberry yogurt.

''I want to believe you're right, and in my heart, I know you are. I resented my father's authoritarianism, but the spiritual truths I learned as a child are still ingrained in my mind. I've become cynical, but it's only skin-deep.''

''Since you believe that, you're well on your way to recovery.''

Joseph didn't speak again as he slowly scraped the last of the yogurt from the plastic container and picked up an apple. Connie welcomed the silence, for it gave her time to think. Although she'd thought this trip might be a mistake, it had given her important insight into Joseph's character. He finished the last of his apple, and threw the core to a waiting raven that, for the last five minutes, had been hopping from one branch to another in a nearby tree, noisily making his presence known.

Without meeting Connie's eyes, Joseph said, "You mentioned guilt—I feel no guilt about the automobile accident. My wife had been injured, the telephone lines were down because of the blizzard, and I was trying to take her to the hospital. The truck crossed the center line and hit our car. I couldn't have avoided any of that."

Obliquely, Connie glanced at her watch. They should leave soon to give Joseph time to rest before dinner, but this informal session might be Joseph's most beneficial therapy, so she shifted her position on the narrow bench and listened intently.

"However, Virginia and I had been growing apart for a long time, and I let it happen. I feel guilty about that. I should have worked harder to make our marriage succeed." He sighed deeply. "It's too late to do anything about that, so I should let it go, but I can't seem to."

"You might remember this Scripture verse from your childhood. 'Forgetting what is behind and straining toward what is ahead, I press on toward the goal to win the prize for which God has called me heavenward in Christ Jesus.'"

He smiled grimly. "Yes, I remember that verse. It was easy to memorize the words, but it's difficult to accept them as a rule for living."

"We can't change the past, as much as we might like to. Can't you try to forget what happened and look to the future?"

"I intend to try, but it won't be easy. What about you?" he continued, eyeing her skeptically. "Can you unload baggage from the past that's troubling you?"

"As of now, I have. That sermon I preached to you found lodging in my own heart. I'd been debating a decision, but I've made it. No more vacillating." The conversation had progressed into ticklish matters, and Connie started gathering up the picnic items.

"We should start back. I have some office work to finish, and you may want to swim or rest before dinner, depending on how you feel."

Rubbing his leg, Joseph said, "Right now, I want to rest, and I doubt I'll have changed my mind when we get back to NLC."

Joseph's leg had stiffened during the leisurely hour they'd enjoyed, and it took a lot of maneuvering to seat him on the four-wheeler. Sensing his discomfort, Connie drove slowly, but she heard him stifle a groan when she hit the brake quickly to avoid striking a deer that ran across the trail. When they arrived at the dorm, Connie turned off the engine and hopped off the ATV. Joseph stared at her, a ludicrous expression on his face, and he made no move to step down.

"Connie, I've always considered myself a level-headed person, and I can't imagine why I ever consented to go riding on this ATV. The pressure on my body as we came down that trail has numbed my left leg. I can't move.''

In spite of being alarmed at his statement, his perplexed expression amused her, and she grinned.

''I've doubted myself ever since I suggested the picnic. As your trainer, I should have known better. Do you suppose we have a bad effect on each other?''

He laughed. ''That's possible, but I can't stay on this ATV the rest of my life, and I can't move. What are we going to do?''

Contrite, Connie trotted to the other side of the ATV and started massaging his leg.

''At least, there's some small gain—when the leg is numb, it doesn't hurt,'' Joseph said, still chuckling over his predicament.

They were startled by Dr. Alexander's booming voice. ''What are you two doing?'' He towered over them, his face black as a thundercloud.

''Joseph and I went on a picnic to Paddy's Point, and he can't get off the ATV.''

Joseph flexed his leg. ''It's better now, but, Doctor, I need some help dismounting. I've had less trouble getting off a bucking horse.''

Dr. Alexander was a tall man, and as Connie supported and protected Joseph's leg, the doctor lifted him off the ATV.

''Walk around and see if you notice any problem,'' the doctor commanded.

Connie took Joseph's arm, and walking with his cane, he said, ''No worse than it was yesterday.

''In spite of the discomfort, I did enjoy the picnic,'' Joseph said. ''I admitted a few things I haven't been able to put into words before.''

"That's good. Mutual understanding is important between a trainer and patient. Try to get some rest before dinner."

Joseph was already in the cafeteria when Connie entered the next morning, and Rose Nash sat beside him. Since they were deep in conversation, Connie waved and moved on to sit beside Kim and Eric.

"How's your new patient doing?" Eric said.

"We start therapy this morning, and for the first time in my career, I'm afraid of failing."

"Isn't it too soon to consider that?" Eric asked.

"Of course, but I feel we're Joseph's last hope, and if I can't help him, where else can he turn?"

Eric laughed lightly. "How about God? He's our ultimate help. If we encourage Joseph to trust in God, regardless of his physical problems, all will be well."

Connie flushed. "That was a careless remark for me to make. For a moment, I forgot the major emphasis here at NLC."

"Eric," Kim said, "perhaps you can befriend Joseph and help him with his spiritual problems."

"I'll do that, of course, because it's my job, but I also want to do it for Joseph's sake. He strikes me as a man with a lot to offer others, and we need to work toward his complete healing."

Eric was an important addition to NLC, having joined the staff during the year. A slender man, with prematurely graying hair, his black eyes revealed not only his Creole heritage, but also his intense passion to help others mature spiritually.

Joseph finished eating before Connie did, and he stopped by their table.

"Meet me in front of the dorm in a half hour," she said.

"Good," he answered. "That will give me time to change into exercise clothes." He lifted his hand in understanding. Connie soon finished her meal, deposited the tray on the rack near the kitchen and left the cafeteria. Ray Blazer was waiting for her beside the door.

"When are we going to talk?"

"Now is as good a time as any," Connie answered. She walked away from the building, and when they were out of hearing of those leaving the dining hall, she said, "I will not resume our relationship. I'm happy this way—our engagement was a mistake, but I hope we can still be amicable associates. It isn't good for NLC when we're at odds."

"You're sure you want it that way?" he asked angrily.

"Yes."

"What if I tell you I'm leaving?"

"I don't want you to resign, but that decision is up to you. If tension between us affects the health of our patients, it will be best for you to leave."

"So I'm good enough to manage your gym, but not good enough to marry," he retorted angrily.

Ray stalked angrily toward the gymnasium. Another chapter in her life closed. "Forgetting what is behind and straining toward what is ahead…" Turning toward the dorm, she noticed that Joseph sat on a bench in front of the building, looking her way. Why did she mind that he'd witnessed her encounter with Ray?

She smiled at him. "Ready?"

"No, I haven't been to my room. I had to rest."

Contritely, she said, "I hope that trip on the ATV didn't add to your discomfort."

He shook his head. "Not at all. My injury isn't any worse, but the least amount of exertion saps my energy."

"Rest as long as you want to—we aren't on a tight schedule this morning."

When Connie left her room a half hour later, Joseph wasn't in sight, but he soon joined her, dressed in denim shorts, a green knit shirt, and sturdy walking shoes.

"Good choice of clothing," she said approvingly. "Let's go this way." She directed Joseph along a smooth-surfaced, shaded walk behind the administration building. Connie wore khaki shorts and shirt, and a water bottle hung at her waist.

"This is our easiest walking path," she explained, "We have three other trails requiring various degrees of physical skill, and the test of your graduation from NLC is to climb Faith Mountain."

Connie matched her steps to Joseph's slow gait, and when they were out of sight of the buildings, she said, "Now, give me your cane."

He paused, startled. "I can't walk without it."

"Have you tried?"

"Only a few steps without holding on to something."

"You must start depending on your own strength instead of the cane."

His facial muscles contracted into grim lines, and the skin whitened around his lips. He struggled with fear.

"What if I fall and end up worse off than I am now? I had a few nasty spills in the hospital when I was in therapy."

Connie understood his hesitancy, for she remembered how frightened she'd been to trust her own strength when she was a child. "I can't guarantee that you won't fall, but I'll walk beside you, and you can put your hand on my shoulder and lean on me."

He handed her the cane, and she tucked it under her left arm. "Just swing your arms slowly and walk as naturally as you can," she encouraged. He took a few experimental steps, and pain etched deep lines on his face.

Connie laid a hand on his shoulder, and her pulse quickened at the touch. You're a trainer—he's your patient! she reminded her heart. "I know that must hurt dreadfully," she said, "but you have pain when you walk with the cane, don't you?" He nodded and gritted his teeth. "There's a bench up ahead. Look toward it as your goal—you can sit down as soon as you reach it."

Joseph moved forward slowly, but relentlessly, and occasionally he grunted in pain. Once he stumbled, and Connie's right arm circled his waist. "Put your arm on my shoulder now," she commanded.

With her support, he walked the rest of the way and collapsed on the bench. Tears of pain and distress seeped from his closed eyelids. Connie sat beside him, took a towel from her pocket and mopped perspiration from his face. She placed the water bottle in his hand.

"Take a drink when you feel like it."

With his eyes still closed, he lifted the bottle to his

lips and drank several long gulps. Water dribbled down his face, and Connie wiped the drops from his chin.

Joseph's heart pounded, and he knew the extra stress wasn't all a result of the exercise. First, Connie's arm around his waist, and now her gentle touch when she wiped his face, drove a small wedge in the barrier he'd built around his heart. Considering the problems he faced, the barrier had to remain intact, but it had been a long time since anyone had fussed over him, and her kindness soothed his troubled spirit.

"I'm so ashamed," he said. "I haven't been this weak since I was a baby. I've never depended on a woman for strength since my mother cut the apron strings."

"I told you it's sometimes necessary to change trainers. Some men resent taking help from a woman. It will be no problem to assign a man to take over your program."

His eyes popped open. "I didn't mean that. It's humbling for me to depend on *anyone*. I want you to continue."

"I wanted to give you a choice, but you must learn to trust me. I won't ask you to do more than you're capable of doing. One of the first steps in healing is to admit you need help and can't handle your situation alone."

He closed his eyes again. "I trust you."

"But you must also trust God." He didn't respond.

Connie massaged Joseph's neck and shoulders and waited for him to find the courage to go on, looking with pleasure around the little glade where they sat. The trail at this point was overhung by huge spruce trees, and a patch of wild roses bloomed in a sunny spot. Pink flowers grew in clusters on the young branches. A downy woodpecker, oblivious to their presence, dug in a tree trunk for insects. She'd always enjoyed this spot, but it seemed even more precious today, and looking at Joseph, she reluctantly admitted the man by her side had made the difference.

Joseph breathed deeply, and Connie thought he slept, for he jumped when a Steller's jay flew into the tree above them, announcing its arrival in strident tones.

Joseph stirred and opened his eyes. "Shall we go on?" he asked reluctantly.

Connie grinned at him. "You don't sound very enthusiastic about it, but I would like for you to continue to the next resting spot. If you make a round-trip to that point, you'll have walked a quarter of a mile."

He struggled to his feet, his hand on her shoulder. "It feels like a streak of fire is running up and down my leg, but I'll try to make it to the next bench." He peered at her. "If I can't make it on my own, will you carry me back to the dorm?"

She smiled at him. "I won't have to carry you. You'll manage. Do you want your cane?"

"Not yet."

Connie laid the cane on the bench. "I'll leave it here until we come back."

He looked longingly at the cane, but with an effort, he started walking. "It gets easier after I've taken a few steps."

He arrived at the next bench without falling, but

each time Joseph stumbled, he grabbed Connie's shoulder with such force that she knew she'd have a bruised spot. He gasped for breath when he dropped heavily on the bench, and Connie feared she might have pushed him too far. She grabbed his hand to monitor his pounding pulse, but when she checked it a few minutes later, it had slowed considerably. She gave him a chocolate bar.

"Joseph, drink more water and eat this chocolate— it will give you quick energy."

He drank deeply, nibbled the chocolate, and with amusement in his gray eyes, he murmured, "Would you believe that the past few minutes I've wanted to hit you?"

"Perfectly normal reaction," she said lightly, "and does no harm, as long as you don't hit me. Right now, I'm your persecutor instead of a helper. But I don't want you to overdo, and if you can't walk back, I'll go for the golf cart."

He shook his head stubbornly. "I'm going to walk back if it kills me."

"Which it won't do, but you may wish for death by the time you reach the dorm. Finish the chocolate, and when you're ready, we'll start."

They reached the first bench without incident, and Joseph grabbed his cane and leaned on it. He didn't rely on the cane entirely as they returned to the dorm, but having it in his hand seemed to be reassuring. Connie went with him to the door of his room.

"Rest as long as you want to," she said, "but I want you to spend a little time in the pool. The warm water is therapeutic."

* * *

"Did Joseph survive his first walk?" Kim asked when Connie entered the office.

"He had a difficult time, but he's determined, and I believe he'll make it. He was exhausted when we got back to the dorm."

Connie thought about Joseph all afternoon, and when he didn't show up at the cafeteria for dinner, she waited fifteen minutes and asked Eric if he'd check his room. Had she pushed him too far? She fidgeted with her food until Eric returned with Joseph. They came to the table where she sat with Kim.

Sleepy-eyed, with his long brown hair falling forward over his forehead, Joseph said, "I'm sorry, but I've been asleep all afternoon—I didn't even go to the pool as you told me to."

"It's probably my fault," Connie apologized. "I may have pushed you a little too far, but I'm eager for you to regain your strength."

He patted her on the shoulder. "I'm eager to improve, too, so don't hold back on my schedule. I'll fill a tray. I'm hungry, so I suppose that's a good sign."

"I need some dessert and a cup of decaf," Eric said. "I'll join you." Connie watched the two men, noting that Eric stayed close to Joseph's side in case he needed help.

Under her breath, Kim muttered, "If that man killed his wife, then I'm a Caribbean pirate." Connie nodded in agreement.

Eric carried Joseph's well-loaded tray back to the table.

With a smile, Joseph said, "Look it over, Doc, and see if I've chosen the right things."

"Anything we have in our dining room is acceptable," Connie said primly, "so eat a lot."

"Have you lost much weight since your injury?" Eric inquired.

"About fifteen pounds—I haven't had any appetite." His facial muscles tightened, and Eric changed the subject.

Now that she knew Joseph was all right, Connie finished her dinner, and she remained with Joseph after Eric and Kim left.

"Is there a romance blooming between those two?" Joseph asked.

Connie nodded happily. "And I'm pleased for both of them. Kim and I have been friends since we were in elementary school, and we shared an apartment when we attended college. Eric came to NLC a year ago from Louisiana. He's had pulmonary problems, and his doctors recommended a higher altitude. He's been fine here in Colorado. They're both wonderful people, and I hope they decide to marry."

"How about you, Connie? I notice your hands are ringless, so apparently you aren't attached."

Connie ate the last spoonful of mixed fruit, wondering what she should say, or if she shouldn't answer him at all and thus adhere to NLC's policy of maintaining an impersonal level between patient and trainer. Already she'd stretched that rule, yet it was hard to be objective when Joseph turned eloquent gray eyes in her direction, and his lips curled upward in a captivating smile.

"No, I'm not attached, and I intend to stay that way."

"There's more to a balanced life than physical fitness, you know, if I can dare to advise my physical therapist.''

Connie stacked her empty dishes on the tray, preparing to leave. ''If you can manage at all, I still recommend that you spend some time in the pool. It will relax your muscles and make tomorrow easier.''

Joseph wasn't easily swayed from his purpose, and wishing it didn't matter so much, he persisted, ''I saw you with NLC's strong man this morning. I sensed an undercurrent in your relationship—something stronger than usual among business associates.''

''Joseph, do you want me to ask questions about your past?''

He colored and refused to meet her eyes. ''Point well taken. I won't meddle again.''

''Since you aren't meddling, I'll tell you what everyone else knows. Ray and I were engaged, but I broke the engagement a couple of months ago. He isn't happy about it.''

''Why?''

She stood up, tray in hand. ''Why did I break the engagement or why isn't he happy?''

''It's pretty obvious why he'd be unhappy to lose you.'' Connie's heart did a little somersault at that comment, for his words applied soothing oil to her ego, which had suffered since her estrangement from Ray. ''Why did you break the engagement?''

''He and I disagree on some things very important to me.'' She walked away from the table. ''Have a nice rest.''

Connie went directly to her apartment and stayed there. She didn't want to encounter either Ray or Joseph again that evening. She was in bed when Kim came in from her date with Eric, but she wasn't asleep. Listening as Kim softly hummed a love song, Connie sensed her happiness, and she tried to remember if she'd ever had the kind of love for Ray that Eric and Kim shared. If she had loved him, would she have been relieved now that they were no longer engaged?

And why did she think about Joseph constantly? She'd worked with many personable men, and while she'd been just as interested in their physical progress as she was in Joseph's, she'd never lost any sleep over them.

Lord, she prayed, *don't lead me into this temptation. After my disappointment with Ray, I don't need to get involved with anyone else. Should I assign another trainer to work with Joseph? That might be the logical answer.*

Tomorrow was her night to visit her parents, and although she wouldn't mention her fascination with Joseph, once off the grounds of NLC and back in her childhood home, she'd be more likely to focus on the proper perspective in dealing with a male patient.

Chapter Four

Connie slept intermittently, and dawn found her dull and sluggish, but she hoped her daily two-mile jog would renew her stamina.

Joseph's sleep was troubled, too, and he sat beside the window, watching, when Connie came outside to wait for Peggy. She wore red shorts and a white shirt. Suddenly the early-morning calm was shattered by a cheerful melody. Joseph identified the rapid melodic chirp of a yellow warbler, and he saw it perched above its nest in the fork of a small tree. Connie must have heard it, too, for when she knelt on one knee to retie her shoe, she lifted her head suddenly, and Joseph saw the joy on her face as she delighted in the songster. He'd never known anyone with such a keen joy of living, and another wedge lodged in the barrier around his heart.

Connie looked upward and saw Joseph watching her, and she waved. He wished he could join her, but he'd made up his mind yesterday that there would be no more self-pity. He'd do his best to overcome his physical problem, and he was confident that he could. But, if not, he would still live a worthwhile life.

He planned to ignore his fascination with Connie, though her past engagement to Ray Blazer bothered him more than he wanted to admit. Was she still in love with Ray?

Connie was in the dining room when Joseph entered. He'd been in the chapel for morning worship, but she hadn't talked with him. He walked to her table. "Do you mind if I join you?"

"Of course not. Sit down. How did you sleep?" she inquired, hoping he wouldn't continue his interrogation of the previous day.

"Not soundly—that long nap I had yesterday afternoon ruined my sleep. I'm determined to stay awake today."

After he gave his order, Connie asked, "How do you feel?"

"My leg is as stiff as a board, but I believe it's stronger. I went to the pool last night as you suggested, and that relaxed the muscles. So, what's on the program for today?"

She grinned. "More of the same. Walking and swimming, with some time in the gym, preferably on the stair-steppers or skate machine."

"You're a hard taskmaster, Doc," he said grimly, but she knew he was joking.

After eating, they left the cafeteria together. "I have to work with Kim in the office for a little while this morning. Take an hour's break before we start walking."

When they started out later, Joseph's steps were slow, and he leaned heavily on the cane. Connie didn't encourage any conversation, preferring that he remain silent and retain his energy for the trail. She didn't ask for the cane, but when they reached the first stop, Joseph hung it on the back of the bench, and he didn't sit down to rest.

"Keep your strong shoulder handy, Doc, in case I have to lean on you. I intend to reach the quarter-mile marker before I turn around."

Connie patted her shoulder. "It's at your disposal. You can even cry on it if you want to."

"It may come to that. I could have bawled like a baby when I got back to my room yesterday. Tears of frustration more than anything else. I'm tired of being disabled."

Joseph moved forward quickly, obviously trying to force strength into his leg, but he soon limped again. When they reached the next marker, he sat down with a heavy sigh. He took a long swig from his own water bottle, which he'd brought along today.

"We aren't in any rush, Joseph. Take all the time you need to rest."

He closed his eyes without comment. A pleasant breeze wafted down from the mountains, and the evergreens sighed above them. Connie loved the scent of the tall spruces, and their carpet of brown needles added buoyancy to her steps.

"You have a great area for your work, Connie," Joseph said. "Quite an undertaking for a woman as young as you."

"I'm almost thirty, in case you're trying to find out," she answered with a grin. "It's fortunate that I could buy this place completely furnished. The price was reasonably low, although it was still a high price for me. I inherited enough from my maternal grandmother to make a down payment on the property, and I borrowed the rest of the money. So far, I've been able to keep up the payments, but it hasn't been easy.''

"I know what you're going through. When it's a poor crop year, I have trouble making the semiannual payment to my parents, and in order to keep modern machinery, I have to borrow money occasionally.''

Connie smiled. "But I have a great staff, and we offer a good program, which produces results, so we never lack clients.''

Joseph put his hand on her shoulder for support as he stood. "Let's go on—the sooner I walk this half mile, the sooner I can rest,'' he said lightly.

Once, on the return trip, Joseph almost fell, but Connie grabbed him quickly and guided him off the trail, where he slumped against a tall spruce to take the weight off his leg. Sweat popped out on his forehead, and she feared he might faint. She wiped his face, murmuring encouragingly, "Only a few more feet before we reach the bench. Take deep breaths.''

His pulse raced at an alarming rate, and his body trembled, but slowly his breathing normalized, and he stood erect.

"For a minute, I thought you'd lost me, Doc.'' He shook his head. "I've never fainted.''

He stopped talking, set his teeth determinedly and walked back to the dormitory without his cane.

"Set the alarm, so you won't miss lunch,'' Connie cautioned when he started to his room. "A proper diet is just as important as physical exercise.'' He nodded, incapable of speaking.

After resting for an hour, Joseph forced himself to leave the bed to keep an appointment with Eric. He took the elevator downstairs and walked slowly toward the chapel, where he found the chaplain in his small office. Eric sat behind a paper-littered desk, and he motioned Joseph to the chair opposite his. The only other furniture in the room was a set of shelves filled with books.

"Come in, Joseph," Eric said. "What did you want to talk about?"

Stifling a groan when he sat down, Joseph said, "I want you to tell me how to get rid of the wall of guilt that separates me from God."

Eric's eyes were compassionate as he said, "What makes you think there's a wall?"

"Because when I read the Bible and try to pray, I don't feel anything. Once I had a close relationship with God and knew that He not only heard but answered my prayers. Now, I feel like there's a burden on my back, and I can't get rid of it."

Briefly he explained to Eric how he had once lived in close fellowship with God, but how he had strayed away during his marriage. He confessed his guilt over the circumstances leading to Virginia's death.

"What are some of the Scriptures you've been reading?"

"One that sticks in my mind constantly is a passage from the book of Isaiah, 'Surely the arm of the Lord is not too short to save nor His ear too dull to hear. But your iniquities have separated you from

God; your sins have hidden His face from you, so that He will not hear.' ''

"It's true that unconfessed sin does hinder the answer to our prayers, but it seems to me that you're open with God about your guilt feelings. God is always ready to forgive, but it may be that you aren't ready to receive His forgiveness. Instead of dwelling on Bible verses that seem to indicate God won't answer prayer, I'd rather you remember words from another Psalm. 'He does not treat us as our sins deserve or repay us according to our iniquities. For as high as the heavens are above the earth, so great is His love for those who fear Him; as far as the east is from the west, so far has He removed our transgressions from us.' ''

Joseph's eyes brightened. "I had forgotten that biblical promise, although I often heard it quoted from the pulpit when I was a child. Perhaps I've been blaming myself for events that I couldn't help."

Eric nodded in agreement. "Let me suggest another Scripture for you to read. Every day, read Psalm 25 as a prayer of confession and petition until your burden is lightened so you can pray. God wants to be in fellowship with those who seek Him. He won't turn you away."

When he went back to his room, Joseph turned to Psalm 25, and hope returned when he prayed, "Look upon my affliction and my distress and take away all my sins.... May integrity and uprightness protect me because my hope is in You."

It was NLC's policy for each staff member to spend a full day away from the Center every week, as well as occasional free evenings. Each Friday night, Connie visited her parents, and she was always eager to see them.

Considering her emotional upheaval with Joseph, today she wanted to see them more than usual. Before dinner, she changed into a white cotton blouse, a long denim skirt and white sandals. She buttoned a red sweater around her shoulders. When she arrived in the dining room, Joseph was seated with three other male clients, so she didn't join him.

Connie ate with Kim and Eric, and when she finished the main course, she said, "I won't get dessert because Mom always has a treat ready for me. She says a fattening dish once a week won't hurt me, and I agree with her."

"If she has chocolate pie, don't forget me," Kim said.

Joseph joined her as she left the dining room. He didn't have his cane, but she didn't comment. He shuffled his feet slowly, but he went with her to the lot, where the NLC van was parked beside his truck.

"I'm going to see my parents this evening," Connie said. "They live in Lakewood."

She got in the van, turned the ignition and nothing happened.

"Not again!" she muttered.

"Out of gas?" Joseph asked. "Or do you want me to check under the hood?"

"No, I know what's wrong. We've had trouble with the starter, and the mechanic put in a rebuilt one, which didn't help at all. By trying to save money, I'll end up spending more." Disappointed, she jumped out of the van. "I'll telephone my parents to tell them I won't be there tonight."

He reached in his pocket and handed her a key. "Take my truck. It hasn't been moved for several days, so a run into Lakewood will be good for it."

"Oh, I won't do that. I don't like to drive someone else's vehicle. If I damage it in any way, that would be another debt for me to pay."

"Then let me drive you to your parents and pick you up when you're ready to leave. I have a friend in Lakewood, and I can pay him a visit."

An alarm sounded in her brain. Remembering some of Ray's actions, she wondered how far she could trust Joseph. After Ray had overstepped the bounds of decency and had forced his amorous caresses on her, she'd become uncomfortable when alone with any man except her father, Eric and Dr. Alexander. As long as she had the comforting arms of NLC wrapped around her, she felt safe, but taking off with Joseph in his truck at night was a different matter. She hesitated, finally answering, "I can go tomorrow night after we have the van repaired. I won't impose on you."

"It isn't an imposition. I've had my swim for the day and spent an hour in the gym, so my evening is free."

She agreed reluctantly, but with a flash of pleasure because they could share some time together unrelated to their trainer-patient relationship. He opened the door for her, and hitched slowly to the driver's side. As they left the parking lot, Ray watched them from the steps of the dining hall.

You've really blown it this time, Connie! For all

anyone knew, she was ignoring NLC's personnel policy and going off for an evening with Joseph—a man
she'd known only a week. She'd probably hear about
it at the next board meeting. They passed Eric and
Kim strolling toward the lake, and she said, "Stop a
minute, so I can tell Kim about the van."

An amused expression crossed Kim's face when
she saw Connie and Joseph together.

"What's up?" she asked.

"The starter won't work on the van. Joseph's giving me a lift into Lakewood. Will you telephone the
mechanic first thing in the morning and tell him we
need a new starter?"

"Sure," Kim said, winking. "Have fun—don't
wake me when you come in." Connie frowned at her,
but that didn't erase the laughter from Kim's eyes.

"If it's convenient for you, come back for me in a
couple of hours," Connie said when Joseph stopped
in front of her parents' one-story brick home. As she
walked up the sidewalk, the lights were still on in the
beauty parlor adjacent to the house, and Connie
turned in that direction. Beverly Harmon sat at a desk
balancing her accounts.

"Hi, dear," she said, and came around the desk to
kiss her younger daughter. "I've just finished. Come
on in the house."

Beverly turned off the lights, and they walked
down the small hallway that connected the shop to
the rest of the house. Bill Harmon was watching a
basketball game on television, and he muted the
sound.

"How's my girl doing?" he asked.

Bill sold farm and ranch equipment, and he was often away from home overnight. Connie was always disappointed if he was gone when she came for a visit. He was a patient man, and even more than her mother, he'd encouraged Connie throughout difficult times. In looks, Connie was more like her mother, rather than her short, brawny father, but in temperament, she took after Bill.

"I had to hitch a ride into town. The starter on the van is on the blink again." She sat on the couch beside her father, and he gave her a hug.

"I saw you get out of a pickup. Are you dating Ray again?"

"No. I'm definitely through with Ray. Besides, he has a Jeep, not a truck. I rode in with one of my patients, who's visiting friends in town. He'll come back for me in a couple of hours."

Connie hesitated to tell her parents who she'd come with, for no doubt they'd heard of Joseph and his troubles. She hoped she could avoid mentioning his name, but her mother said, "Who, Connie? One of your regulars?"

"No. Joseph Caldwell has been at NLC less than a week. You may have heard of him."

"I know Caldwell," Bill said. "He's been a customer of mine. I've sold him several pieces of machinery. Why would he be at NLC?"

"He came for physical therapy. He hasn't recovered from an automobile accident he had a few months ago."

Beverly took the platform rocker beside the couch and slowly rocked back and forth, her brown eyes questioning. "Joseph Caldwell! I've heard something about him." That didn't surprise Connie, for besides what she may have heard on television, Beverly's clients carried lots of news to her door. "Wasn't his wife killed in that accident?"

"Yes, and the authorities aren't convinced that her death was an accident. Joseph is suspected of doing away with his wife. We had some dissension on the board about accepting him, assuming it wouldn't be good for NLC's reputation, but he needs therapy to walk as he did prior to the accident, and we think we can help him."

"You made the right decision, Connie," Bill said. "Caldwell is a good man, and I'd never suspect him of wrongdoing. Hard on his reputation, though."

"From the few things he's said, I believe he's suffering from mental anguish as well as his physical injury." She turned to her mother. "Kim said to send her some dessert—that is, if you've prepared any."

Beverly smiled happily. She liked to have her culinary arts appreciated. "It's a refrigerator dessert— Cherry Delight—but I'll put a serving in an insulated bag for Kim, and it'll keep until you get back. Let's wait until Mr. Caldwell returns, and invite him in for a snack."

"Thanks, Mom. He's had a rough week."

Joseph returned promptly two hours later, and when he rang the doorbell, Connie greeted him.

"Come in, Joseph," she said, opening the screen door. "My dad says you're a customer of his, and Mom wants to give you some dessert."

Bill had followed Connie to the door. "Good to see you again, Mr. Caldwell."

"Bill Harmon! I hadn't connected you and Connie. I knew you lived in the Denver area, but I didn't know where."

"This is my mother, Beverly," Connie said when they walked into the family room. Joseph's left leg wobbled, and Connie remembered that he hadn't brought his cane when they left NLC. She wanted to reach out and let him lean on her, but she suspected he wouldn't welcome her help.

"It's nice of you to give Connie a lift tonight, Mr. Caldwell. I'll reward you with some dessert before you go home."

"And we'll have to leave soon, Mom, because I have a heavy schedule tomorrow and I'll need a good night's rest."

"Come in the kitchen, and I'll have it ready in a few minutes."

Joseph held on to the furniture, and Connie could tell it was an effort to refrain from groaning each step he took. His face registered surprise when he sat at the table and saw the huge serving of Cherry Delight that Beverly placed before them. Connie looked in dismay at the new dessert her mother had made—a crumb crust of nuts and pastry, a heavy layer of cream cheese and whipped topping, covered with fresh cherries smothered in a sweet glaze.

"I assume all of the calories have been taken out of this, Mrs. Harmon." With an impish grin at Connie, Joseph added, "I've been placed on a strict diet."

"You can use a few calories," Beverly said. She patted Bill's ample stomach. "We can't all be muscular like Connie. Besides, she doesn't always practice what she preaches."

"That's no way to encourage my patients, Mom."

The half hour passed quickly because Joseph and Bill discussed Colorado's ranching industry. Beverly had a knack for putting guests at ease, and people always enjoyed visiting the Harmon home.

"Come back any time, Joseph," Beverly called to them as they left the house.

"If my diet at NLC is too restrictive, look for me at your door often."

As they walked toward his pickup, Joseph said, "Connie, will you drive? I hate to admit it, but I'm in so much pain, it isn't safe for me to be behind the wheel. The pickup shouldn't be any more difficult to drive than your van."

"Why didn't you tell me you were hurting? We could have gone back as soon as you came to the house. I'm sorry."

"Don't be. I enjoyed meeting your parents. It's a surprise to learn I know your father. I've always liked him, but we haven't been well acquainted."

"They've given me lots of love and security. Without their encouragement, I wouldn't be where I am today."

"I can tell they're good parents."

As she drove the truck out of town, Connie said, "It might be good for you to see Dr. Alexander in the morning before we go walking. I can understand your joints being stiff, but you shouldn't be in a lot of pain."

Joseph laid a warm hand on her shoulder, and Connie trembled at his touch. Hopefully, he hadn't noticed. "Don't fret about it. I'm to blame. I should have stayed in my room and rested tonight, but I still won't admit that I can't do the things I've done all of my life. And, of course, I had to leave my cane behind! I have a bad case of male ego. A night's rest will do wonders for me.''

When they parted at the door of Connie's apartment, he said, ''I had a good time, Connie, so it was worth the price I had to pay. The pain has lessened considerably since I didn't have to drive home. I'll be all right in the morning.''

''I enjoyed the evening, too,'' she said, although she wished it wasn't so.

At the end of two weeks, Joseph could walk two miles slowly on the easy trail, but still with a noticeable limp. He wasn't easily discouraged, but there were days, when the pain was severe and his strength unequal to the task, that he shed tears of disappointment. During those dismal times, Connie said very little. He had to fight some battles alone. Beginning his third week, Connie started Joseph on the second trail, which required more stamina because it wound uphill part of the way, and the round-trip was three miles.

At the end of each month, Dr. Alexander gave every client a thorough checkup, the trainer made a detailed report, and the staff members who'd worked with the client submitted a progress report to the board. After these individual evaluations, the patient met with the board members.

It always thrilled Connie when someone she'd worked with for a month was evaluated, especially when there was a marked improvement, as in Joseph's case. When he walked into the conference room without a cane, still with a slight limp, but with buoyancy in his step, Connie felt like shouting, but she prayed instead.

Oh, God, why is he so important to me? I don't want to love him. But Connie suspected that her greatest fear had already happened. How could anyone spend the better part of a month with Joseph and not love him? He had a keen mind and an engaging personality that drew people to him. Connie wondered how much the residents at NLC knew about the cloud hanging over Joseph, for without putting forth any effort, Joseph had become popular with the other NLC patients, as well as with the staff. He and Della were great friends. Eric had become as fond of him as if they were brothers. Kim had been Joseph's champion from the first day, and she was aware of his past. If he was a favorite with everyone else, it was small wonder that he'd wiggled his way into Connie's heart. She admired him especially when he was most vulnerable. Only Connie had witnessed his vulnerability—those times when he couldn't walk any farther, when his leg hurt until he cried out in pain, or when discouragement plagued him.

When Joseph sat at the conference table, Eric said, "Congratulations, Joseph. All reports indicate that you've made a lot of progress in the last month. Your recovery thus far is certainly above average."

Obliquely, Connie glanced at Ray. He was the only person at NLC who hadn't accepted Joseph, but to give him credit, he had rated Joseph well on his gym performance. He didn't continue to let personal bias influence his professional behavior. That was one thing in his character Connie could admire.

Flashing a grin in her direction, Joseph said, "I've had a good trainer."

Pleasure brightened Connie's face. "Thank you, but the credit has to go where it's deserved. Unless the patient is determined, a trainer can't do much."

"How do you feel about the program, Joseph?" Eric asked. "How do you evaluate *us?* Have we met your expectations?"

"Quite frankly, I didn't anticipate much when I came here. Dr. Melrose told me NLC was my last chance, and I was desperate enough to try anything. So, yes, NLC has more than met my expectations, and more important than my physical improvement, I can hope again—I have a confidence in the future that I haven't had for a long time." He paused as if to summon his courage. "And, Eric, much of that has come from attending your chapel services. My parents were conservative in their religious views, and I know the Bible well because I was required to memorize portions of it in my childhood, but I've sparingly applied biblical principles to everyday living. Being here at the Center has turned my whole life in a new direction."

Speaking of being vulnerable! Connie had never been so incapable of controlling her emotions. It was a good thing Eric chaired this meeting, for she didn't want attention focused on her. What might her face reveal? If she wasn't under the watchful eyes of her staff, she would probably round the table and throw her arms around Joseph. Knowing him had enriched her own life. To avoid looking at Joseph, she glanced to the left and met Ray's cynical eyes. *He* knows! she thought.

"We're happy you're improving, Joseph," Eric said. "The board is in full agreement that you should continue your therapy, and it sounds as if you're of the same mind."

"Absolutely! I intend to climb Faith Mountain before I leave—in more ways than one." Connie sensed he was looking at her, but she wouldn't meet his gaze.

When the meeting adjourned, Joseph joined Connie and Kim as they walked toward the dormitory.

"I'll wait for Eric," Kim said, and she slowed her steps. "We're going to the dining hall for frozen yogurt. Want to come with us?"

Connie and Joseph declined and walked on without Kim.

Choosing her words carefully, Connie said, "You made me very happy tonight. Your personal testimony proves that NLC is doing the work I want it to do."

"Do we have to wait until I climb Faith Mountain before we celebrate? Let me take you out to dinner."

"We discourage social contact between the staff and patients. I wouldn't set a good example by breaking the rule."

"Is that a no?"

Smiling, she said, "For now. I thought you should know why I hesitate. It's not forbidden, but it's probably not a good idea."

"It depends on whose point of view you consider. Personally, I think it's an excellent idea. Will you go?"

Joseph's coaxing voice weakened her resolve.

"Against my better judgment. Tomorrow night is when I visit my parents. We can skip dinner here, eat in town and go to see them. Or I could telephone Mom, and we can eat with them.''

"I'm selfish. I want this celebration between the two of us.''

"We're together most of the day.''

"I know. It's becoming habitual for me.''

Though she felt she was capitulating too easily, Connie said, "We can leave at five o'clock.''

When Kim came in an hour later, Connie sat on the bed in a cotton lilac sleep T-shirt, legs curled under her body, arms behind her head. Kim was radiant, and there was a soft expression in her eyes. How could her friend be so confident and happy, when Connie was so confused?

"What happened to make you glow?'' she said peevishly.

"Eric asked me to marry him tonight, and I said yes.''

Stifling her own frustrations, Connie said, "Oh, Kim, I'm so happy for both of you. Have you decided on a date?''

"No, not yet, but we want to marry sometime this summer.''

Kim must have sensed Connie's dismal attitude, for she looked at her keenly. "I thought you'd be asleep by now.''

Connie shook her head, and was shocked to realize she was on the verge of tears. She hadn't cried since her grandmother's funeral, so why was she weepy now?

Kim sat on Connie's bed. "What's wrong? I thought you'd be on top of the world after the progress Joseph has made. He was surely impressive tonight and gave NLC a good evaluation.''

"He asked me to go out with him for dinner tomorrow night, and I agreed! I can't believe I'd ignore one of the Center's guidelines.''

"Oh, you're the boss—you should have a few privileges. Don't worry about it. Some of the rest of us may have broken a few rules you don't know about,'' Kim said with a smile. "Go and enjoy yourself.''

Kim went into the bathroom, put on her pajamas, and when she returned to the bedroom, Connie hadn't changed her stance. Kim got into the other bed, but before she turned out the light, she said, "Want to talk about it?''

Connie's lip quivered slightly. "I'm upset over the way I feel about Joseph.''

"Be more specific. Are you in love with him?''

"How do I know if I'm in love?''

"I'm no expert on the subject, since Eric is my first love.''

"Well, I thought Ray was my first and *last* love, but my relationship with him didn't prepare me for the mess my emotions are in now. Joseph is in my mind constantly, and I want to be with him all the time. When our hands touch in a casual way, my pulse races. But it isn't only the physical awareness, I just *like,* him—he's pleasant company, and I'll admit that I want to be more to him than his personal trainer.''

"What's so bad about that? We all like him.''

"In the first place, after the heartache over that broken engagement with Ray, I decided I was through with men. Now, only a few months after I stopped dating Ray, I can't get Joseph out of my mind."

"You're with him several hours a day, it's natural you would think about him."

"I've had other male clients who didn't cause a ripple in my composure. Besides, considering the questions about his wife's death, I should be cautious."

"Do you think he's guilty of killing her?"

Connie shook her head.

"Neither do I. Has he told you anything about that?"

"Very little, and I certainly won't bring up the subject."

"I wish I could help you, Connie, but it's a problem you'll have to work out by yourself. Friends can sympathize and encourage, but there's a limit to how far we can go."

"I know. It helps to talk out my frustrations, so thanks for listening. I like Joseph a lot, but I wish I hadn't been so hasty to accept his dinner invitation."

Smothering a yawn, she fluffed her pillow and stretched out on the bed. "See you in the morning, Kim. Thanks for being my friend."

Kim grinned and turned out the light.

Chapter Five

Since she had only a few dressy outfits, Connie dithered most of the day about what to wear for her dinner date. She considered the new dress Beverly had bought for her birthday, wondering if the turquoise column dress was too fancy for the occasion. The scalloped sleeves were decorated with matching rhinestones and faux pearls. An elegant V-back fastened with loops and fabric-covered buttons drew attention to the long back slit. She was pulling the dress over her head when Kim came in.

"Wow!" Kim said, emitting a long whistle. "That's elegant!"

Turning in front of the door mirror, Connie said doubtfully, "I don't know, Kim. It might be *too* elegant. He may intend to take me to a fast-food place. I don't want to overexpect."

"When Joseph sees you in that outfit, he'll take you to a classy restaurant. Wear it!"

With a sigh, Connie said, "I'll have to—nothing

else seems right. After wearing casual clothes most of the time, I'm uncomfortable in dresses.''

"Let me style your hair," Kim offered. She brushed Connie's straight brown hair, used a styling iron to give her fine tendrils a bit of curl and arranged the hair behind her ears.

"Wear those pearl earrings Beverly gave you for Christmas last year, and you'll capture Joseph's heart."

"I'm not sure I want to capture his heart," Connie retorted.

She slipped on a pair of white mesh slides, and took a light jacket from the closet. She stayed in the room until Joseph knocked at the door, hoping the residents and staff would be in the dining room when they left. Though she considered it a cowardly attitude, she didn't want NLC residents to speculate on the importance of this outing.

Even after Joseph knocked, she hesitated. Her appearance this evening was such a contrast to her usual casual attire that she couldn't help being self-conscious. She took a deep breath and opened the door. What if she'd read more into his invitation than he intended?

Joseph stared at her, speechless, for a minute. He wore a light-brown suit, matching silk tie, and a white shirt. "You're a different person, but I like the transformation," he approved, his drawl more pronounced than usual.

"Mother bought this dress for my birthday, and I haven't worn it. She'll be pleased to see me wearing it."

"No more pleased than I am. I feel a little mean

insisting on taking you out for dinner when it goes against your policy at the Center, but let's consider this dinner a part of my therapy. You're supposed to keep your patients happy, you know.''

His affectionate, light tone eased her concerns. Time she spent with Joseph was gratifying, so as they drove toward Lakewood, she took pleasure in his company as she always did. He chose a restaurant Connie hadn't visited, and the carpeted room with private booths, muted lights and soft music lent a romantic atmosphere to their dinner. Both of them ordered seafood entrées.

After they finished eating, Joseph lingered. Her parents would be expecting her, but she hesitated to rush him. Her hand rested on the table, and he covered it with his.

''Connie, how much did you know about me before I came to NLC?''

''Not much. I'd seen you on television a few times.''

''Have you heard anything about the legal problems I'm having?''

''Just a little.''

''Then may I explain? You know my wife died in the accident that caused my injury. It was a bad wreck, so that wasn't surprising, for the doctors said it was a miracle I wasn't killed, too. But when the autopsy showed that she probably died from a blow to the head prior to the crash, my brother-in-law held me responsible and demanded that the police make an investigation.''

''He must have had some reason for the accusation,'' Connie said slowly, voicing a thought that was often in her mind.

"When I came in that evening, Virginia was lying on the floor, unconscious and bleeding from a wound on the back of her head. She'd been drinking heavily the past several months, and I supposed she'd probably passed out and fallen. Our phone lines weren't operating because of the blizzard, and I couldn't call 911, but I knew she needed help. I carried her to the car and we were on the way to the hospital when the accident occurred.

"The day before her death, Virginia had written a note to her brother, George, and I've thought about that note so much the words are etched in my memory. 'He's taken all my money and everything else I have. Now he's threatening to take my life. I don't know what to do.' George jumped to the conclusion that she meant me, and he went to the police with his suspicions.

"For several days after the accident, there was a policeman stationed outside my hospital room.

"The authorities commandeered my ranch and IRS records, and my sister says they snooped around the ranch a lot in the first few weeks. They're still monitoring my bank accounts, they check with my lawyers occasionally to see if I have any proof of my innocence, and pay periodic visits to the ranch. Every time they show up at the ranch, I'm afraid they've found some evidence that will incriminate me.''

"If Virginia didn't mean you, who else could have been threatening her?'' Since he'd brought up the subject, Connie wanted to learn all she could about the incident. She'd wondered often, too often, about Joseph's relationship with his wife.

"I have no idea. Virginia had inherited almost a half-million dollars from her father. I don't know what she did with her money, but not one penny of that inheritance came into my pockets. After she died, I learned that she'd been making large cash withdrawals from the bank for several months. The police might have arrested me if they'd found I'd gotten the money, but my bank accounts have always been sparse. They still think I've got it stashed away, and now that I'm getting well, they'll watch every move I make."

"Her brother must have had some reason to accuse you." A look of pain crossed Joseph's face, and he released her hand. Connie added quickly, "Joseph, don't get me wrong—I don't believe you're the kind of man to do away with your wife, but it's a question many people might ask."

His eyes brightened, and he took her hand again. "Don't think they haven't! Folks I've known for years cross the street to keep from speaking to me. I appreciate your vote of confidence—your opinion is important to me. I've spent months trying to figure out the puzzle. A half-million dollars has disappeared without a trace. I'd just as soon believe she gave it to George as to me, for they'd always been close, but I won't accuse him as he did me. I suppose the authorities have investigated him, too."

The waitress came with their bill, and Joseph placed money in the tray. "We should go—I don't want you to be late for the visit with your parents."

When they were in the truck, he said, "I'll admit

that my spirit, as well as my body, was injured when I came to NLC, but I'm beginning to heal both ways. Yet, I can't quite forgive George for accusing me of killing her. He'd been my best friend for years—it was through him that I met Virginia. To lose his friendship was almost as painful as losing my wife.''

"Perhaps in his grief, he had to lash out at someone, and you were the logical one to accuse. Without that note, would there have been any question that she'd died in the accident? I don't mean to pry, but had you had any marital problems that had started her drinking?''

The dashboard lights illuminated Joseph's perturbed face, and Connie saw him shake his head. ''Not really! We'd been married five years, and the last couple of years we'd not been as happy as we were at first, and at one time, she left me for several months. I decided that was normal, that the honeymoon was over, but my lawyers have been pressuring me to come up with any possible motive. Mrs. Perry died about two years before her husband, and I've decided that Virginia started to change soon after that. I didn't question her attitude, believing it was grief, but after her mother died, instead of turning to me, she became more secretive, went off by herself a lot.''

"That doesn't sound normal—it seems she would have turned to you in her sorrow.''

"It would seem so. But as I've looked back, I realize that was about the time she started drinking secretly. I knew it, but I ignored the habit.''

"Did she inherit any money when her mother died?''

"A few thousand dollars, and that's gone, too. I

didn't question her about what she'd gotten from her family, for George is a better financier than I am, and he was in charge of settling the estate. The Perrys employ several accountants, and I assumed that they were handling Virginia's portion.''

''Perhaps she spent a lot of money on clothes.''

''It's possible that's what happened with the first money she received, but she could hardly have wasted Mr. Perry's fortune so quickly. As I look back, I see now that I should have been more attentive to what my wife was doing.''

''If you find out what she did with the money, that might be a clue to what happened the night she died.''

Joseph laid his arm across Connie's shoulders and drew her close to him, and she looked at him questioningly, but his mind was still on the past. ''I've been immobile so much since the accident that I've had plenty of time to go back over the manner of her death. I'm inclined to think she may have been attacked that day. If someone had been at the house, the blizzard would have wiped out tire tracks. My employees and I had worked all day driving the stock close to the ranch buildings. Virginia had been alone for hours, and from the amount of blood she lost, she might have died even if we hadn't had an accident.''

''So that would have been murder?''

Joseph rubbed his left leg and thigh, a common gesture when he was agitated. ''And while the police persist in suspecting me, the real killer is free. I can't get it out of my mind. Will I have to wonder the rest of my life what really happened and have people suspect I committed the crime?''

Connie laid her hand on his arm, and he covered

her warm fingers with his hand. "I pray not, Joseph—surely the police will uncover something."

"They aren't making an effort. I'm their number one suspect, and they're watching me." Thoughtfully, Joseph added, "Strangely enough, the first bit of evidence we've found, I learned from Rose Nash."

"Rose!"

"You know she worked for Virginia's parents. She told me that sometimes, after our marriage, when her parents were gone, Virginia would come to her former home and stay all night, and that a few times she had a male guest. Rose saw him once, but it wasn't anyone she knew, and she wondered if it was someone she'd met during a year she wandered about the country before I met her. I've hired the best lawyers available, and they're checking into Rose's information, but it's an old trail, and so far they haven't learned anything."

"I'm willing to help if you need me."

"Thanks. Until I get better, I'm leaving the detective work in the hands of my lawyers, but when I'm well again, I'll do some private searching. I may call on you then." He sighed. "The future seems bleak, but I don't know what else to do."

They were turning into the driveway of her parents' home, and Connie squeezed his arm. "There's one big avenue of defense that you may not have tried yet. Prayer! 'If God is for us, who can be against us?'"

He threw her a grateful smile. "Perhaps *you* should pray for me."

"Do you think I haven't?" Without waiting for him to open the door, Connie stepped out on the driveway. "Come in with me. We'll see what mom has for dessert."

Joseph had been at NLC for six weeks—weeks full of triumph for Joseph and Connie as his strength began to return and he learned to walk without a limp. He'd graduated to the third most strenuous trail, leaving only the trek up Faith Mountain to prove he'd mastered his disability. There had been days of disillusionment, too, when Joseph fretted over the mystery of his wife's death, and the lack of evidence his lawyers had been able to find. His recovery hadn't been without pain either, and often after a strenuous day, he couldn't sleep at night. During these times, Connie overlooked his irritability and encouraged him with pats on the back and patient words. Connie had set today for a new test for Joseph. They would jog rather than walk.

When Joseph met her at half-past six, the air was cool and invigorating, and the sun shone brightly.

"I have a surprise for you today," she said. "We'll run part of the way."

Joseph turned skeptical gray eyes on her. "Are you sure I'm ready for that?"

"We'll soon find out. Rather than taking the easiest path, I think you'll be able to run a mile on the second trail. We can slow to a walk when necessary."

He grinned at her. "Okay, Doc, you're the boss, but if my legs cramp like they did last night, I probably won't run far."

They walked to the trail head beside the lake. Mallards and their ducklings paddled away leaving V-shaped wakes behind them. Red-winged blackbirds fussed over their nests in the reeds. A fish flipped, and its body glistened like silver in a ray of sunshine.

When the trail entered the woods, Connie said, "We can't run side by side here, so you go first and set the pace. I'm hoping for a mile each way, but you decide what you can do. We're not attempting a marathon, so it doesn't matter how long it takes."

Joseph still favored his left leg, and at first, he ran awkwardly and slowly, but he eventually picked up speed, although she knew it was an effort. When she thought he'd exerted enough, she hurried forward until she was beside him. His flushed face was set in rigid lines, and his breath came in gasps.

"Don't keep running if you think it's too much. We have another half mile to go, so slow to a walk when you want to."

He shook his head, clamped his teeth in determination, and kept running. Smiling, Connie dropped behind him. When Joseph finally slumped down on the bench at the one-mile marker, he gasped for breath, his face was red and sweaty, his legs shook, but he managed a feeble smile.

"Made it," he whispered weakly.

She wiped his face, and handed him the water bottle. While he drank, she sat beside him and sipped her own water. He rested for ten minutes or more without speaking, while Connie monitored his pulse.

"Do you know you irritate me sometimes?" he mumbled. "I'm ready to collapse, and you look as cool as if you've been sitting in the shade all day. You make me feel inferior."

"Your recovery has been miraculous. There's no reason for you to feel inferior. If you do this every day for a week, you'll hardly breathe heavy at the end of your run.''

"Maybe so," he grumbled. "Right now, I'm not thinking about next week, simply wondering how I'm going to make it back to my room.''

The smile she gave him was warm, compassionate and mysterious, and her charm so captivated Joseph that he spoke without thinking. "Do I get a reward for my accomplishment?''

She reached in her pocket and playfully dangled a granola bar in front of his face. "Okay, here's your reward.''

"That's not what I had in mind." He drew a deep breath and put his arms around her, as she turned startled eyes in his direction. "Do you think I can be with you almost constantly for six weeks without succumbing to your charm? I know it's foolish of me, but I'm jealous of other men who've had you for their trainer—men I don't even know—wondering how they felt about you.''

She thought she'd seen Joseph in all his moods, but she'd never seen his eyes glow with the tenderness they displayed now. When his lips touched hers, at first in a gentle kiss that soon intensified, she eagerly returned the caress. Why pretend she was insulted by his action? Why push him away when her heart overflowed with joy? She had been right to let Ray go, for she'd found in Joseph the tenderness and love she expected in a mate. Connie shifted her face to end the kiss, lowering her head to his shoulder, still damp from the rigorous exercise. She pushed the future with its problems out of her mind. Right now, all she wanted was the joy of being in Joseph's arms.

His right arm held her tightly, and his left hand softly touched her hair. Happiness surged though her body in a vibrant, lovely melody.

Although appalled at what he'd done, Joseph continued to hold her. What was the matter with him? His wife hadn't been dead a year, and here he was kissing another woman. Considering the enormity of the legal problems overshadowing his life, the last thing he needed was to become entangled in a love affair. Was it love? Or was he lonely? What should he do now? He didn't want to offend Connie by shoving her away.

Connie moved out of his arms reluctantly, belatedly remembering that she was the supervisor of his rehab program. This interlude was definitely not on the prescribed schedule. She got up from the bench and turned her back.

"Did I offend you?"

"No," she answered honestly, "but I am surprised that I so easily forgot I'm on duty for NLC."

He tugged on her arm until she sat beside him again and rested her head on his shoulder, holding his hand as she monitored the steady rhythm of his heart and listened to his words.

"I suddenly realize I want more from you than counseling and encouragement. After that kiss, it will be impossible for us to be together so much and keep our association on a strictly professional level."

"This is my fault for breaking one of the main rules at NLC. Trainers aren't supposed to get emotionally involved with their patients."

"But since we're already emotionally involved,

what are we going to do about it?'' he asked, a wide smile creasing his face.

"I don't know,'' Connie murmured, not really wanting to make any decisions. It seemed so right—so comfortable—to be in Joseph's arms that she wanted to blot out the rest of the world for the moment.

"Why don't you go home with me next weekend? We need time to know each other better, and that's hard to do when we're surrounded by so many people.''

"Just the two of us by ourselves?''

"Why not? We're attracted to each other, and we need time alone to see how far we want this relationship to go.''

Connie's heart thudded to the pit of her stomach. What she had regarded as love flowing between them was apparently nothing but lust. Speechless for a moment, she finally lifted her head, looked at him suspiciously and demanded, "Are you suggesting that we start an intimate relationship without being married?''

Joseph's breathing had normalized, but now his pulse raced again, and he felt as if he'd finished a marathon. He hadn't meant that at all! How was he going to answer? If he said no, Connie would be embarrassed that she'd jumped to the wrong conclusion. He certainly wouldn't consider a premarital relationship, but at a loss for words, he shrugged his shoulders and hedged. "It might lead to that eventually.''

When Ray had made a similar proposition, it had angered Connie so much that she'd immediately given him an unequivocal no, and she'd never once regretted her decision. Why was she hesitating now? Did she love Joseph so much that she was actually considering his suggestion?

Appalled at her behavior, Connie jerked out of Joseph's arms and stood up, resembling a wounded animal holding its attackers at bay. In a harsh, angry voice that didn't even sound like her own, she said, "Joseph, do you have any idea why I broke my engagement with Ray Blazer? He suggested that we live together a year or so to see if we were compatible for marriage!" She pointed to the pin she wore every day. "Do you know what this pin means? Haven't you heard that I'm the coordinator of a support group of men and women who believe in, and have taken a Marriage First vow? We've pledged to refrain from sexual relations before marriage, preferring to keep our virtue for our spouse."

"No, Connie, I didn't know any of that."

She was shaking all over, and her voice trembled as she continued, "Now that you do—let me say that you've disappointed me greatly. What have I done or said to give you any reason to believe that I'd consider such an offer? I've certainly set a poor example if you have such an opinion of me." Right now, however, he couldn't think any worse of her than she thought of herself.

"I respect you more than anyone I've ever met. You've taken this all wrong, Connie. I didn't mean to insult you," Joseph protested, and he reached out a hand to her.

"I belong to the Marriage First group because chastity is so rare these days that we need the support of others who are like-minded to avoid faltering in our beliefs." He struggled to his feet and she backed away from him. "You claim to know so much about the Bible, but perhaps you need to be reminded of the words of the Apostle Paul, 'The body is not meant for sexual immorality, but for the Lord.' So, if you still need an answer to your weekend invitation, the answer is *No!*"

Ignoring his protest, Connie broke into a run and scurried down the trail. Once again, she'd forgotten he was her patient, leaving him to get back to the Center on his own.

Connie lay facedown on her bed, exhausted in mind and body. Someone knocked on the apartment door, and she ignored it. The phone rang several times, but she didn't answer. If it was Joseph, she didn't want to talk to him, but probably it was Kim. Connie vaguely remembered that she had an appointment sometime today, and Kim was probably calling to remind her. Then the apartment door opened, and Connie sat up on the side of the bed as Kim entered the bedroom.

"You missed your appointment with the Cartlands at ten o'clock. You were supposed to discuss NLC's services for their son, who was injured in a waterskiing accident. When you didn't show up, I telephoned Eric, and he's taking them on a tour of our facilities and will treat them to lunch. When can you meet with them?"

Connie didn't answer, and Kim sat beside her. "Is there anything I can do?"

Connie shook her head.

"Cat got your tongue?" Kim said with a little

laugh, asking the question they'd often used as children when one of them was mad.

Connie shook her head again.

Kim put her arm around Connie. "Oh, come on, Connie. It can't be that bad."

"It's bad, all right," Connie said grimly. "I'm mad at Joseph and even madder at myself."

"I thought you must have had a quarrel. I saw you racing by the office like a rabbit with a pack of hounds on its trail, and an hour later, Joseph came limping by, looking as if the weight of the world had been dumped on his shoulders."

"A quarrel is a mild word for what happened between us," Connie said, and she stood up and paced around the room. "He insulted me, Kim. He invited me to go with him to his ranch next weekend, so we could 'get to know each other better.'"

"That may have been a perfectly innocent invitation. He's lonely, Connie—maybe he just wanted your company. Was that all he said?"

Connie's eyes widened, and she stared at Kim, her face flushing with embarrassment. Had she misconstrued his meaning? She tried to recall Joseph's exact words. Had she put words into his mouth?

"As troubled as Joseph is over his health and his wife's death," Kim continued, "I don't think he even realizes it, but it's obvious to Eric and me that he cares for you a lot. I've watched the tender expression in his eyes when he looks at you, and sometimes his eyes are wretched as if he knows how hopeless his life is. Then he reminds me of a kid who dreams of owning an expensive toy, but knows his dreams will never come true."

"I know he likes my company, and I'm happy when we're together, but it really upset me when I thought he considered me a fast woman, as my grandmother would have termed it."

"I assume you refused his invitation," Kim said, and her eyes twinkled in amusement.

Connie flushed and dropped down on the bed beside Kim. "Of course, I said no. I was mad at him, but I was angrier at myself because for a minute or two, when I believed he was suggesting a premarital relation, I was tempted. I was tempted! All these months, when I've preached 'marriage first' to our support group, I didn't suppose I would ever consider such an arrangement—not even for a moment."

Kim put her arm around Connie's rigid shoulders. "Connie, you're only human. There's no harm in being tempted since you had the courage to say no. The Apostle Paul commented on that in his message to the Corinthians. 'God will not let you be tempted beyond what you can bear. But when you are tempted, He will also provide a way out so that you can stand up under it.'"

"Perhaps I shouldn't ask, but have you and Eric been tempted?"

Kim blushed, but she met Connie's eyes. "I don't know about Eric, for we haven't discussed it, but there have been times when I've wished we were already married, if you know what I mean, and I haven't felt guilty about it. I had the strength to deny my temptations, and two months from now on our wedding day, we'll be glad we waited."

"You make me feel a little better, Kim, but I'm afraid I made a complete fool of myself."

"Oh. I doubt it was that bad," Kim said. "I must go back to the office. What are you going to do now?"

"Take a shower and try to get my mind settled enough to meet with the Cartlands."

"But what are you going to do about Joseph?"

"I don't know. The way I feel right now, I never want to see him again."

"But you'll have to see him again, and the sooner the better. You'll both be miserable until you talk. Joseph must feel badly about it."

"I don't want to talk to him. I'll assign someone else to be his trainer—I can't possibly work with him now. Regardless of what he meant, we could never achieve the rapport we had before."

"It's your decision, but I think you're being unreasonable. I'm sure he didn't mean to insult you."

Connie was a little put out that Kim championed Joseph's position instead of hers, but she'd already ruined the day by losing her temper with Joseph. She couldn't antagonize Kim, too.

"He said he didn't know about my abstinence convictions. But, regardless, I hadn't given him any reason to believe I would spend a weekend alone with him." But was she being completely honest about that? She hadn't hesitated to accept his caresses, so the fault might be hers as well as Joseph's.

With her hand on the doorknob, Kim said, "I could ask Eric to talk to Joseph."

Connie shook her head. "No, thanks. I'll deal with it some way."

After she showered, Connie dressed in a pair of white denim jeans and a brown shirt. Still troubled in

mind, she bypassed the cafeteria and went to the
chapel. Why did she make such poor choices in the
men she dated? The soft music she heard when she
entered the chapel didn't soothe her spirits as it usually did, but if there was any place she could find
peace of mind, it would be here. Connie stopped
abruptly. Joseph knelt in the front of the chapel, his
head lowered on the altar. Seeing him in this penitent
attitude cooled her anger considerably. She backed
out of the building before he could turn and see her.

Ignoring the pain in his leg and thigh as he grov-
eled on the hard floor, Joseph silently brought his
frustrations to God, who at one time had been his
greatest solace.

"God," Joseph prayed aloud, "I'm ashamed to call
on You when I've ignored You for years, but my life
is in shambles, and I have no other place to turn. I've
always thought I was strong enough to handle anything that came my way without help from anyone,
but I've learned that isn't true. I've spent months in
hospitals and clinics, and even yet, I'm a long way
from recovery."

The wall between Joseph and God seemed impossible to penetrate when he considered the disastrous
scene he'd perpetrated with Connie. Feeling guilty
about his neglect of Virginia when she had apparently
needed so much, he was afraid to become involved
with Connie, so why had he kissed her? Not only did
he feel unworthy of another woman's love, he also
wondered how God could love him.

"God, I'm miserable, and in Your omnipotence,
You know all of this, but somehow it helps to talk

about it. I feel alone, but will You give me some indication that You're with me, that You hear my pleas, and that You still love me in spite of my rebellious ways?"

Joseph sat with his head in his hands, waiting, and God's assurance came soon. Doubts fled and peace flooded Joseph's soul, for in a still, small voice in the deep recesses of his heart, he received the message he needed.

You've never been alone, Joseph. I've been there all the time, even when you didn't recognize my presence. Since that day when you were a boy of twelve, and you invited Me into your heart, I've been with you, and I'll stay with you throughout eternity.

He lifted his head, and his assurance was complete when he remembered the words of a plaque hanging on the wall of his dormitory room. "'But I will restore you to health and heal your wounds,' declares the Lord."

Tears of relief stung Joseph's eyelids, and he prayed again. "What about the future, God? How can I overcome the mistakes of the past? Is there a place for Connie in my life? Is that why You brought me to NLC?" But although he sat with bowed head for a long time, he received no answer to those questions.

Connie avoided Joseph for the rest of the afternoon, but he was on her mind constantly. During her interview with the Cartlands, their son's injury reminded her of the first time she'd seen Joseph. He'd improved so rapidly under her guidance, how would it affect him if she refused to work with him any longer? After the Cartlands left, she stayed in the office, trying to work, but spent most of the time staring out the window, wondering what Joseph was doing. When dinnertime came, she knew she couldn't stay hidden any longer, and she walked with Kim to the cafeteria. Joseph's truck wasn't in the parking lot. Had he left NLC?

She and Kim sat with several other staff members at a large table. Eric and Joseph came in together, and Connie saw that his limp was more pronounced than it had been for days. His gray eyes sought hers, and their glances locked momentarily. The men took seats behind Connie, and she was relieved she didn't have to look at Joseph. Had he told Eric what had happened? She hoped that none of the staff or patients had detected a rift in their relationship. It was bad for morale when a conflict surfaced. Everyone had been edgy for several days after she'd broken her engagement with Ray, and she didn't want to cause any more unrest. The Center would never be any stronger than its leader.

As soon as she finished eating, Connie excused herself, took her tray to the kitchen, and went back to her apartment. She paced back and forth in the small area, praying for direction. She paused abruptly when a knock sounded at the door. Convinced it was Joseph, she considered ignoring the knock, but she couldn't run from him forever, so she opened the door.

Joseph's shoulders slumped, and he favored his injured leg. He stared at her from wretched gray eyes, and a muscle throbbed in his forehead.

"This has been the longest day of my life. I've never spent such a miserable time—none of the days

I was in the hospital can compare with what I've gone through today.'' He reached a trembling hand toward her. "Will you give me a chance to explain?"

Hot tears stung Connie's eyes, and her throat was too tight for words. She took his hand in hers, and he squeezed her fingers until she winced from the pain.

"Let's take a drive, get away from NLC for a while. There are too many interested eyes here."

She nodded and closed the apartment door behind her. In silence they walked to his truck, and not until they'd driven through the entrance gates did Connie remember that she had avoided being alone with Ray after he'd transgressed. Did that indicate she trusted Joseph more than Ray?

Joseph drove along the river for a short way, and stopped when they came to a level area sloping down to the stream. He lowered the windows, and a cool breeze grazed Connie's face. The nearby river gurgled as it bounded over the rocky bed and settled into a serene pool below a miniature waterfall.

Staring straight ahead, Joseph said, "I suppose the first thing I should do is apologize. You don't know how many times today I've wished I could live this morning over and take back my careless words. I can't do that, but will you believe that I wish I hadn't said them?"

"Yes, of course," she murmured.

"I spent some time in the chapel this morning, asking God to forgive me for what I'd done to you. I invited you to the ranch on the spur of the moment, and I shouldn't have."

"Oh, Joseph," Connie said with a sob. "Let it go. I shouldn't have gotten so angry, but I was disappointed in you, as well as in myself. If I hadn't been so receptive to your advances, you wouldn't have made your suggestion. It's my fault as much as yours, or perhaps even more. I broke the rules of NLC by dating you, and I'm suffering for it now.''

"But I didn't have anything immoral in mind. You jumped to the wrong conclusion, and I went along with it.''

"Let's just forget it.''

He shook his head. "I can't forget it, and neither can you.''

"I'm going to appoint a new trainer for you—someone who will remember what NLC stands for.''

"If you don't continue as my trainer, I'll leave,'' Joseph said slowly.

"But you're not ready to leave yet,'' Connie protested. "You've done so well. I don't want you to lose what you've gained.''

"I can't help that. I suppose I'm too proud to start with another trainer, when the other patients will know we've quarreled. I can't blame you for not wanting to work with me, but I don't want anyone else.''

"I'm not sure we can work together now—our emotions may get in the way again, and that isn't good for your health.''

He laid his hand on her shoulder, but when she flinched, he removed it.

"When I sat on that bench this morning, exhausted from my jogging, I hadn't thought of doing what I did. But as I rested, with my eyes closed, and you were holding my hand and wiping my face, it came over me how bleak my life has been for the past year, and I compared it to the serenity and peace I have with you. I don't know what the future holds for us, but I can't let you go out of my life completely, and that's what will happen if I leave NLC.''

Connie swallowed another sob and moved closer to him. He took her hand. "Even if you had gone to the ranch with me, I'm sure nothing wrong would have happened. Besides your Marriage First vow, I don't believe that type of behavior is right, either. I respect you for your stand, for I consider abstinence the test of true love. If I ever marry again, I'd want a wife who'd saved herself for me.''

"Don't say any more, Joseph. I'm not angry now, but considering my own reaction to your caresses, it seems better for you to have another trainer.''

He shook his head stubbornly. "The real test of love is trust. Test me, Connie. I promise I'll never tempt you to forget your principles.''

"Things can never be the same between us again.''

"Give me another chance. I can't prove that my motives are genuine unless you trust me again.''

"I should apologize to you for misinterpreting your intentions. After my experience with Ray, I'm suspicious of any man—I'm afraid to trust them. You haven't given me any reason to believe you're dishonorable. The fault is mine. I'm not ready to trust my heart to anyone.''

"I've felt the same. The last two years of my marriage weren't particularly satisfying as I've told you, and I never intended to become romantically involved again. That changed when I met you.''

Connie sighed. "Right now, Joseph, the most important thing is your health. If we can put this morning's incident in the back of our minds and concentrate on your healing, I'll go ahead. Just this one incident has set you back—you're limping again and you'd almost overcome that. I'll have to treat you like any other patient at NLC. We can't have a repetition of what happened this morning.''

"You have my word. I'm not sorry I kissed you, but I won't kiss you again unless you ask me to. Does that satisfy you?''

With a grimace, she moved away from him. ''Not particularly, but that's the way it has to be.''

He started the truck, turned around and headed toward NLC. When he parked in front of the administration building, he asked, ''Does our restricted involvement mean I can't take you to dinner or go with you to see your parents?''

Connie hesitated. She wanted to be with Joseph, but she questioned that they should have anything to do with each other outside the confines of NLC. If Joseph was attracted to her, was it right to put temptation in his way? On the other hand, if she avoided him, he might think she didn't have the strength to keep her abstinence vow.

''I can't give you an answer now, Joseph. Let me think about it. We'll continue jogging in the morning, but not on the trail by the lake. Try to get a good rest tonight.''

After a few days, most of the strain wore off, and for long periods, Connie forgot the misunderstanding with Joseph. As his strength returned, he spent a lot of time in the gym, and he progressed more rapidly than she'd expected. He could jog two miles now without any effort, and they left the dormitory at six o'clock each morning. On the last Friday in July, when they stopped to rest before they returned to the Center, Connie said, "You're two weeks ahead of schedule, Joseph, and ready for Faith Mountain now. I want to start climbing on Monday morning, going farther each day, and you should be able to make it to the top by the end of the week."

"If I remember, when I'm able to do that, you'll turn me loose, huh?"

"Yes, although you should continue exercising. Is there a gym near your home where you can work out? Your muscles will become flabby if you start riding horses and traveling in pickups without any body-building exercises."

"There's not a gym close, but I'll buy an exercise machine. The lawyers haven't taken all of my money yet."

"Have you heard anything more about this mysterious stranger your wife was seeing?"

He shook his head. "I'm going home tonight, and I'll be in touch with my lawyers. I hope they have some new leads."

"I hope so, too."

He pulled up a tuft of weeds at his feet. "Are you still thinking about whether to date me?"

She'd wondered why he hadn't asked again, but she was reluctant to mention it.

"I suppose it will be all right."

He grinned mischievously. "Good. How about going home with me next weekend?"

"What!" she shouted, but returned his grin when he added, "I want Kim and Eric to come, too. I'll ask my sister to be there as hostess. My ranch is east of Fort Collins.''

"I don't like for the three of us to be gone at the same time, but if the others agree, I'll ask my parents to stay at NLC for the weekend. Dad could keep his eye on everything and telephone if I need to return. Della Sinnet will be pleased to conduct the worship services in Eric's absence. If he and Kim accept your invitation, I'll be happy to come. I'd like to see your ranch.''

"Good. I'll talk to Kim and Eric before I leave tonight. I've learned so much about your way of life during the past three months that I want to introduce you to my world. And, too, I want to take you up on your offer to help me solve the mystery of Virginia's death. We'll need to start at the ranch, and this visit will be a good time for you to look around.''

"I'd like that. And I'm sure Kim and Eric will enjoy the visit.''

He stood up and stretched. "But I have to climb Faith Mountain before that, so we'd better jog back to the Center.''

Chapter Six

By Wednesday, Joseph had climbed three-fourths of the way up the mountain, so Connie said, "Are you ready to try for the top? I think you can make it tomorrow." Although she rejoiced over Joseph's improved health, Connie wasn't as happy as she should be. When he reached his goal, he would leave NLC, and she would miss him.

"I think I can, too. I'm ready! The ranch needs its owner."

"Eager to leave us, are you?" Connie said, without looking at him.

"You know better than that! But I have a ranch to manage. I have several good employees, but the boss still needs to be at home."

"We'll eat an early breakfast and leave the Center at eight o'clock. I'll ask Rose to pack a lunch for us. The last part of the climb is steep, and we'll need to rest before we start home. It will take most of the day."

Joseph reached out his hand and pulled Connie to a standing position, and he put his arms around her in a brotherly hug. "It feels great to be the one helping you for a change! A few weeks ago, I thought that day would never come. It's a good feeling."

The Marriage First support group met the fourth Wednesday night of each month in the lounge of the administration building. Since its organization two years ago, the group had grown from a handful to over fifty members. Although all the members didn't attend regularly, Connie, Kim and Eric made it a point to be present for each meeting.

Tonight, thirty people sat around the room when Connie arrived. Their schedule didn't vary much. Each meeting opened with prayer and a Bible study led by various members. The purpose of the group, repeated at the close of the Bible study, had been formulated into a pledge of three sentences, and each member committed the lines to memory.

I believe my body is the temple of the Holy Spirit. If I defile my body with immorality, I dishonor the Spirit of God living within me. Therefore, I pledge to maintain the purity of my body until my wedding day. Marriage First!

The agenda of each meeting was similar. Most of the evening was spent in sharing experiences, with some members giving testimonials of how they'd overcome temptation, while others asked for prayer to deal with a current problem.

Tonight, Eric conducted a Bible study on the liaison between King David and Bathsheba, citing the many problems that arose from their stolen love, primarily the murder of Uriah, Bathsheba's husband, and the death of David's son born to Bathsheba. The penalty of his indiscretion followed David throughout his life when one son seduced his half sister and was killed by the girl's full brother, Absalom—the beloved son who later revolted against David and tried to take his kingdom. The problems that plagued David and Bathsheba vividly illustrated the results of immorality.

The evening proceeded as usual until the testimonial time when Laura Filkins, a woman who'd been in the group only a few months, said, "People, I hate to burst your bubble, but I've broken my pledge."

Connie gasped. They'd never had a defector before. Everyone must have been too stunned to answer for silence greeted Laura's remark.

Laura lived in Littleton and came to work out in the gym several times each week. Other than that, Connie knew nothing about her. "And I haven't been completely honest with you. I infiltrated your little group to see what you were doing, and it's been interesting, but you people are certainly naive. Loosen up and live a little! Why suffer for an ideal that's impossible to achieve?"

Having dropped her bombshell, Laura rose languidly and strolled from the room, but Connie followed her, catching up with her outside the building.

"Why, Laura? Why did you do it? No one pressured you to join us—you came of your own free will. I'm sorry you don't share our beliefs, but why try to belittle what we're doing?"

"Curiosity, I suppose. Ray and I have been friendly for years, and I find him quite captivating. I was curious as to why you'd reject him, although personally, I'm glad you did."

Anger consumed Connie for a moment. "Do you mean that Ray continued to see you even when we were engaged?"

"Well, yes, you could say that."

Connie was stunned, but she didn't doubt the truth of her words. Too heavyhearted to comment, Connie watched Laura stroll to her car, unconcerned that she'd left behind a group of people to doubt their own strength to overcome temptation. But when Connie returned to the lounge, Eric had drawn the group together, and they were praying—some on their knees—asking for strength to persevere in spite of criticism, scorn and temptation. Was it possible that Laura's words would strengthen the convictions of the rest of them? During times of persecution, the Church had always grown. Perhaps what she now considered a catastrophe might strengthen the support group. This thought bolstered Connie's low spirits, but her morale was shattered because a man she'd once loved had deliberately plotted to wound her.

Kim and Eric stayed behind with Connie when the others left, and she told them what Laura had said about Ray.

"I'm sorry, Connie," Eric said.

"I can't imagine how I could have been so blind in my choice of the man, not only as a fiancé, but also as manager of the gym. This situation forces my hand. I'll have to ask for his resignation. I can't have someone on the staff who's undermining the work we're trying to do.''

"Is he under contract?''

"Yes, the same as everyone—a year at a time— but I think his present contract expires in a couple of months. Perhaps if I tell him I'm not renewing his contract, he'll leave before then.''

"I'll sit in with you when you talk to him, if you'd like,'' Eric said.

"Yes, please,'' Connie accepted his offer. "I want a witness to our discussion. I'm a little afraid of him.''

"And with reason, I think,'' Kim said. "I'd hate for him to be my enemy.'' Eric flashed a warning look at Kim.

"I'll plan to meet with him next week. I can't to-morrow, for that's when Joseph is scheduled to climb Faith Mountain. It will be an all-day trip, and one I've anticipated with pleasure, but tonight's incident has been so upsetting, it'll keep me from rejoicing in his accomplishments.''

Mulling Laura's revelation over and over in her mind, Connie couldn't sleep until after one o'clock, and she felt sluggish when she met Joseph in the lobby of the apartment house. They both wore cleated hiking boots and denim shorts, but Connie had put on a white sweat top, and Joseph wore a plaid cotton shirt. She carried a wide-brimmed hat, and he had a blue baseball cap perched on his head.

They went to the cafeteria for a light breakfast and to pick up the lunch Rose had prepared for them.

"If you make it to the top and back,'' Rose said

to Joseph, "I'll bake the chocolate-pecan pie you like. I still need to search through that box of recipes."

"If I graduate," Joseph said, "I won't be back next week, so you'd better find it today."

"I hope you can reach your goal," Rose said, "but we'll miss having you around here."

They divided the lunch and placed the food and a supply of water in each of their backpacks.

"Rose always prepares too much food, and it becomes burdensome before we reach our destination," Connie said, "but it does taste good when we settle down for our picnic on top of the mountain."

The atmosphere was nippy, but bright sunlight, promising a pleasant day, generated steam from the dew-covered grass. Connie breathed the fresh air deeply and took the lead when they came to the trail head.

"Call out if you want to rest," she said and started off at a rapid gait, but after warming up for a mile, she slowed down.

The trail wound around the mountain through a forest of juniper, fir, and pine. Logs, lying across the trail, provided hurdles to test the dexterity of the hiker. Once out of the forest, the trail crossed a rock slide area leading to a steep climb that dropped into a drainage area, followed by a two-mile ascent that leveled off when it entered a grassy meadow. After that, a half-mile slope that was almost perpendicular had to be scaled before hikers reached the summit with views west to higher mountains and east to the plains.

On Monday, Joseph had climbed to the rock slide; the next day he'd continued and scaled the first steep incline; Wednesday, he'd made it to the grassy meadow. The perpendicular climb was the final test, which he would attempt today. When they came to the rock slide, the sun beamed down on their backs, and the warmth was welcome after the deep shade of the evergreen forest.

"I'm climbing up the mountain where the sun shines all day long; my heart is full of happiness, and I praise God with a song." Joseph sang loudly, surprising Connie with his mellow baritone. "Do you know that little chorus? I learned it years ago when I attended Bible school."

"Yes, I know it, but I'm saving my breath for climbing," Connie answered shortly.

Joseph laughed. "Are you hinting that I'm going to need a lot of breath before we reach our destination?"

Connie grinned at him over her shoulder. "You'll see."

"I thought of the Bible verse, 'The mountains and the hills shall break forth before you into singing, and all the trees of the field shall clap their hands.' The sighing of the evergreens, and birds singing in the forest sounded like music to me. I just had to lift my voice in praise, too." He clapped his hands vigorously.

Connie didn't answer.

"You're awfully quiet today," he said, and when she still didn't answer him, he said in mock penitence, "Since singing isn't acceptable, is it all right if I talk?"

She nodded, and he continued, "It's strange how our priorities change through the years. When I was a kid, I resented the time I spent in church and reading the Bible, but since I've been at NLC, my whole attitude has altered. I've recalled scores of Bible verses Dad forced me to learn.''

''I'm happy to hear that. Everybody needs a well-rounded life to be physically and spiritually whole.''

They had made only two rest stops, and Connie was exhausted and hot by the time they reached the grassy meadow. Breathing was always more difficult at this altitude, and she glanced over her shoulder to monitor Joseph's progress. He was several yards behind her, walking more slowly than he had at first, but he wasn't limping. He lifted a hand, indicating he was all right.

A small stream flowed lazily through the grass, and Connie knelt beside it in a patch of yellow arnicas and red monkey flowers, dipped her hands in the icy water and washed her face. A few yellowbells still bloomed—their golden flowers mingling with vast patches of blue gentians. A meadowlark perched on a swaying reed, filling the air with its musical song, and a female mountain chickadee protected her nest with snakelike hissings, while her mate attempted to distract the visitors with its cheerful chatter. Bleached trunks of fir trees dotted the area, and a herd of deer stopped grazing to twitch their ears and stomp their front hooves at the intruders. Usually this area brought peace of mind to Connie, but not today, for her thoughts were on the pending interview with Ray.

Joseph's face flamed when he reached her side, and he gasped for breath. She hurriedly got to her feet and removed the pack from his shoulders.

''We'll stay here at least an hour,'' she assured

him. "And we'll have a snack to give you enough strength to make it to the top."

Joseph sprawled in the grass without answering, and she sat beside him and lazily sprinkled some of the cold creek water over his face. He licked the cool water from his lips.

"What if I can't make it up the last incline?" he gasped.

"You'll be all right after we've rested. I'm about bushed, too."

While Joseph rested his body, his mind remained active. He was climbing Faith Mountain! Wondering if he had the stamina to reach the top, he compared this experience to his spiritual climb, which hadn't been without problems, either. Under the guidance of his parents, as a teenager, he'd accepted Christ as his Savior and he had grown in the faith. Even when he left home for college, he still trusted God to guide him. When had he stopped forging upward in his Christian climb? He easily traced the decline of his spiritual journey to the time he became involved with the Perrys. His parents had warned him that he would sacrifice his spiritual priorities if he married into their family, but he'd loved Virginia and hadn't heeded the warning.

How different would his life have been if he'd chosen another mate? He looked at Connie, as she stretched out on the ground, and wondered.

Connie willed her throbbing muscles to relax, but her riotous thoughts gave her no rest. Try as she would, she couldn't get last night's meeting out of her mind. She lay, eyes open, staring at an occasional thunderhead that blocked the sun's rays. Quick showers were common at this height, but these clouds didn't seem ominous. She lay quietly because she thought Joseph slept, and she didn't want to disturb him.

When she heard him stirring, she glanced his way. Joseph, leaning on his elbow, looked toward her.

"Are you mad at me, Connie?"

Startled, she sat up quickly. "Of course not! What gave you that idea?"

"Something's wrong. You're different today than I've ever seen you. I thought I might have offended you."

She shook her head. "No—it's a personal matter. There's no need to bother you about it."

"Tell me," he insisted. "Anything that concerns you concerns me."

She opened her backpack and took out a container of trail mix and two bottles of pink grapefruit drink. "Here, take a little refreshment. We'll need it before we reach the top."

"Will you tell me what's bothering you then?"

"Have you had experiences that you don't want to talk about?"

"Lots of them, but, if they weighed on my mind, I believe I could share them with *you.*"

He didn't push for an answer, and they ate in silence. After the snack, Joseph went through a series of stretching exercises to limber his joints. "We might as well go, Doc. I dread what's ahead of me, and I want to get it over with." He flashed a frown in her direction. "After today, I don't ever intend to climb again."

"That will be up to you. Once you've reached the

top of Faith Mountain, my supervision ends. I will have done all I can for you.''

''Ah, my dear, you know better than that,'' Joseph said.

Connie flushed, but wouldn't meet his eyes as she fastened her backpack. Another black cloud hid the sun.

''We should have brought ponchos,'' she said. ''I've been watching these clouds—we may have a shower.''

She started walking, and Joseph fell in behind her. She prayed silently, *Lord, give him the strength to climb the mountain. He's worked so hard, and I don't want him to fail this last test.*

At a small wooden shelter near the foot of the steep incline, Connie picked up two walking sticks, and handed one to Joseph. ''These help,'' she said. He looked upward, a helpless expression in his eyes. He took the stick, but didn't comment.

Joseph kept doggedly at her heels, and she stopped often to catch her breath. He breathed deeply when they stopped, but he didn't speak, and she knew the light air at this altitude was overworking his lungs. Once he slipped, and she looked back quickly. He didn't fall, but a look of pain crossed his face, and she hoped he hadn't hurt his hip.

At the end of a quarter-hour, they were still climbing. When Connie topped the summit, Joseph wasn't far behind, although she sensed he had about reached the breaking point. She removed his pack, took his arm and eased him to the ground. He lay with his eyes closed while she massaged his leg and thigh, and his body slowly relaxed under her hands. He opened his gray eyes, and he took her hand.

"I made it!" he said. "I passed the test. You're a good trainer, Doc."

"Joseph, I'm so happy for you. You've made a remarkable recovery." Impulsively, Connie leaned forward and kissed his lips. His surprised gray eyes held hers captive, and he drew her close for a few minutes.

Irritated at her action, she pulled away from him, and he said teasingly, "There wasn't anything in our agreement that said you couldn't kiss me."

Connie flushed and wouldn't meet his gaze. "I didn't intend to do that—it just happened," she apologized.

"Hey! I wasn't complaining. Now it's my turn."

Joseph's legs might have been weak, but there was nothing wrong with his arms, and he pulled Connie against his chest, close enough that she felt the rapid thumping of his heart.

"You have to ask me."

Aggravated at herself for initiating the situation, Connie said grumpily, "Okay, kiss me!"

Their eyes locked for a few moments before he put a hand behind Connie's head and pulled her lips to meet his. Joseph's weariness disappeared like magic, and when Connie responded to his touch, he felt as if he could have climbed Mount Everest.

Connie quickly put some distance between her and Joseph. She'd never experienced anything like that. How could one kiss make her feel as light as one of the clouds above her? To get her mind off of her reaction, Connie stood and glanced at the sky. "I promised you some food when we got up here, but I don't like the looks of these clouds. There may be a storm. Can you make it back to the shelter before we eat?''

"I'm not hungry," he said, struggling to his feet, "but, rain or not, since I've finally reached the top of this mountain, I'm going to enjoy the view before we start down. I'll probably never come up here again."

They slowly circled the narrow point. Below them, the buildings of NLC resembled a miniature town. Denver, to the east, was easily recognizable, and an airplane flew over them on its descent into the international airport. Westward and northwest, the rugged mountains straddling the Continental Divide glowed in the midday sun. A pair of eagles, taking advantage of the air currents, hovered over their heads.

"Let's picnic here," he said. "That storm is passing north of us."

Connie agreed, and they emptied their packs of the items Rose had sent along. Slick slices of roast beef on rye bread, peaches, small tins of baked beans and a sack of chocolate chip cookies.

"A meal in the finest restaurant couldn't beat this," Joseph said, and he took the last bite of his peach and reached for a bottle of water. "A climb like that is enough to give a man an appetite."

"How much weight have you gained since you came to NLC?"

"Ten pounds—and it's all muscle, thanks to you. I'll have to watch my diet when I get home. I'll need a cook. Could I steal Rose away from you?"

"I hope not. She's the best cook we've had."

"So, do I leave in the morning?"

"We'll have your goodbye party at noon in the cafeteria, but you can be on your way soon after that. We like to recognize achievement, for it helps the other patients to see that healing is possible."

"I have an appointment with my surgeon tomorrow afternoon. I'm anxious for his report."

"The staff at NLC will want a report from him, too."

She started to pack their lunch, and he stopped her by taking her hand. "Tell me what's bothering you."

Taking a deep breath, she said, "I have to ask for Ray Blazer's resignation, and I dread the confrontation." Briefly, she told him about the disastrous Marriage First meeting the night before. "I only hope that Laura's attitude won't discourage our other members. We meet for support and it was a close-knit group until Laura came along."

"I'm sorry, Connie. I really am. Is there any way I can help you with Ray?"

"No. It's something I have to do, but Eric is going with me when I talk to him." She shook her head in frustration. "I can't believe I was such a poor judge of character and I failed to recognize the kind of guy Ray really is. I actually considered marrying him!"

"It's easy to misjudge people. When we rested in the meadow, I wondered what my life would have been like if I'd chosen a different wife. Virginia left me for several months, and she would have divorced me then, but I'd taken her for 'better or worse,' and she was insecure, so when she wanted to come home, I agreed. I still blame myself for not trying to help her work out her problems. But that's in the past, and

Get 2 Books FREE!

Steeple Hill® publisher of inspirational Christian fiction, presents

Love Inspired®

a new series of contemporary love stories that will lift your spirits and reinforce important lessons about life, faith and love!

FREE BOOKS!
Get two free books by best-selling Christian authors!

FREE GIFT!
Get an exciting mystery gift absolutely free!

To get your 2 free books and a free gift, affix this peel-off sticker to the reply card and mail it today!

Get 2

HOW TO GET YOUR
2 FREE BOOKS AND FREE GIFT

1. Peel off the 2 FREE BOOKS seal from the front cover. Place it in the space provided at right. This automatically entitles you to receive two free books and an exciting mystery gift.

2. Send back this card and you'll get 2 Love Inspired® novels. These books have a combined cover price of $9.00 in the U.S. and $10.50 in Canada, but they are yours to keep absolutely FREE!

3. There's <u>no</u> catch. You're under <u>no</u> obligation to buy anything. We charge nothing – ZERO – for your first shipment. And you don't have to make any minimum number of purchases – not even one!

4. We call this line Love Inspired because each month you'll receive novels that are filled with joy, faith and true Christian values. The stories will lift your spirits and gladden your heart! You'll like the convenience of getting them delivered to your home well before they are in stores. And you'll like our discount prices too!

5. We hope that after receiving your free books you'll want to remain a subscriber. But the choice is yours – to continue or cancel, anytime at all! So why not take us up on our invitation, with no risk of any kind. You'll be glad you did!

6. And remember…we'll send you a mystery gift ABSOLUTELY FREE just for giving Love Inspired a try!

Steeple
Hill®

SPECIAL
FREE GIFT!

We'll send you a fabulous mystery gift, absolutely FREE, simply for accepting our no-risk offer!

©1997 STEEPLE HILL

Books FREE!

HURRY! **Return this card promptly to get**
2 FREE books
and a
FREE gift!

Love Inspired®

YES, send me the 2 FREE *Love Inspired* novels and FREE gift, as explained on the back. I understand that I am under no obligation to purchase anything further.

Affix
peel-off
2 FREE BOOKS
sticker here.

NAME	(PLEASE PRINT CLEARLY)

ADDRESS

APT.#	CITY

STATE / PROV.   ZIP/POSTAL CODE

303 IDL CQEK   **103 IDL CQEL**
                                    (LI-LA-01/00)

Offer limited to one per household and not valid to current
Love Inspired subscribers. All orders subject to approval.

Steeple Hill Reader Service™—Here's How it Works:

Accepting your 2 free books and gift places you under no obligation to buy anything. You may keep the books and gift and return the shipping statement marked "cancel." If you do not cancel, about a month later we will send you 3 additional novels and bill you just $3.74 each in the U.S., or $3.96 each in Canada, plus 25¢ delivery per book and applicable taxes if any.* That's the complete price, and — compared to cover prices of $4.50 in the U.S. and $5.25 in Canada — quite a bargain! You may cancel at any time, but if you choose to continue, every month we'll send you 3 more books, which you may either purchase at the discount price...or return to us and cancel your subscription.

*Terms and prices subject to change without notice. Sales tax applicable in N.Y.
Canadian residents will be charged applicable provincial taxes and GST.

If offer card is missing write to: Steeple Hill Reader Service, 3010 Walden Ave., P.O. Box 1867, Buffalo, NY 14240-1867

BUSINESS REPLY MAIL
FIRST-CLASS MAIL   PERMIT NO. 717   BUFFALO NY

POSTAGE WILL BE PAID BY ADDRESSEE

STEEPLE HILL READER SERVICE
3010 WALDEN AVE
PO BOX 1867
BUFFALO NY 14240-9952

NO POSTAGE
NECESSARY
IF MAILED
IN THE
UNITED STATES

I'm moving on in spite of that mistake. You can do the same with Ray.''

"I know, but it isn't easy to admit you've had faulty judgment.'' She stood up. ''Your hard climbing is over,'' she said, ''but the trip down the mountain is the most treacherous. That's where your walking stick comes in handy. It provides another leg for you, and you'll need it.''

"I'll be careful. I can't handle another fall right now.''

Their descent to the grassy meadow was made without incident, and after a short rest, they moved onward. They had almost reached the forest when, without warning, it started to rain.

"What do we do now?'' Joseph shouted.

"Keep walking and get wet. There's nothing else we can do.''

Connie had been hot from the walk off the mountain, and when the cold rain pelted her body, steam rose from her clothes. When she reached the cover of the forest, she kept walking for fear of a lightning strike. Soon the rain stopped and the sun illuminated their path.

Grinning, she turned and faced Joseph, who was shaking water from his cap, and wringing water out of his shirttail.

"Did you order that little shower?'' he demanded.

"No. But it will help you remember your trek to Faith Mountain.''

"I wouldn't have forgotten it anyway.''

When they stopped for a rest, Connie said, ''Since you live in the Fort Collins area, perhaps you'd like to participate in our yearly wagon train trip. For three

years, in the last week of August, we've sponsored a
wagon train trip into Roosevelt National Forest. We
could use an experienced rancher along.''

"I might be able to go. I've fished and camped in
the forest.''

"The trip is organized by a commercial camping
outfit. They provide the horses, wagons, tents and a
few experienced guides. Our people do the rest of the
work.''

"How many usually go along?''

"Between twenty and thirty. We close NLC for a
week, and we take any of the staff and patients who
want to go. If staff members don't like camping, they
can have the week free. Some patients are furloughed
to their homes.''

"I'll think about it and tell you when you come to
the ranch next weekend.''

The joy of achievement gave Joseph added energy,
and he kept pace with Connie's long-legged stride as
they returned to the Center. Dr. Alexander and Peggy
were leaving the administration building when Connie
and Joseph entered.

"I made it,'' Joseph shouted, and Dr. Alexander
grabbed his hand and shook it vigorously.

Peggy smiled broadly and gave Joseph a hug. "We
knew you would,'' she said. "Congratulations!''

Connie and Joseph hurried on down the hallway to
share their good news with Kim.

The following morning Connie watched from her
office as Joseph carried his belongings and packed
them in his truck. Three months ago, he hadn't been
able to carry his luggage into the room. What a dif-

ference those months had made in his life, and hers. She hated to see him leave, the days ahead loomed bleak and lonely. Last night, as she waited for sleep, she knew that she loved Joseph. But as long as he was under suspicion for murder, what future did they have? Until that situation could be resolved, they had to remain friends, nothing more.

For the farewell dinner, Connie wore an ankle-length, belted khaki twill shirtdress and brown sandals. She wanted Joseph to remember her in something besides sweats and shorts. The kitchen staff had prepared roast turkey, potato casserole topped with corn bread dressing, green beans and garden salad. Instead of the fruit plate that everyone else had for dessert, Rose brought in a large chocolate-pecan pie for Joseph, and in her boisterous manner, she called, "Don't look, Connie," as, with a flourish, she placed the pie in front of Joseph.

Connie joined in the laughter. "I hoped you wouldn't find that recipe."

Taking advantage of the general gaiety, Rose leaned over Joseph. "I found something else, too. Be sure to see me before you leave."

Joseph cut the pie into small pieces, and shared the pastry with all the people at his table. When dessert was finished, Connie moved to a podium near the kitchen door.

"If you'll come forward, Joseph, we have a gift for you." It took all of Connie's willpower to handle this ceremony in an impersonal way. She had considered asking Eric to emcee, but she'd always presided before, and the patients might question why she didn't.

Joseph left his chair easily, all trace of his injury gone.

"Before you leave Joseph, we want to recognize your outstanding achievement by giving you this plaque." She handed him a topaz-blue marbleized plaque mounted on a walnut-tone board, with yesterday's date, and an inscription lettered in gold: "On the above date, Joseph Caldwell completed NLC's rehabilitation program by successfully climbing Faith Mountain."

Below these words, a Bible verse had been inscribed, "Your faith has made you whole."

"In addition to the plaque," Connie continued, "you're leaving with our best wishes for the future. You've made a remarkable recovery, bringing satisfaction to all the staff here at NLC. Thanks for trusting your body to our care."

Joseph took the plaque from Connie and they shook hands. He looked at her, and although he spoke to the group, the message his eyes conveyed was for her alone. But she had to guess at the interpretation.

"I leave here a wiser and healthier man. I'll always be grateful to Dr. Melrose for recommending NLC to me. At first, I resented the strict curriculum, especially the enforced chapel services, but I soon learned that the spirit must be healed before the body is restored. Here at NLC I've rediscovered the God of my childhood, and I've renewed my commitment to live as He'd want me to. I appreciate your concern for me, and the prayers all of you have said on my behalf. Thank you."

Most of the people came forward to shake hands with Joseph, but Connie noticed that Ray slipped out the door, reminding her that she would have to deal with him the first of the week. When most of the staff and patients had gone, Joseph said quietly, "I'd like to see you alone for a few minutes before I leave."

"Okay, I'm going to the office."

"I'll be along as soon as I see what Rose wants."

Connie walked back to the office with Kim. "I'll miss him," Kim said.

"We always miss our patients when they've been here as long as Joseph has."

"But he's special," Kim added with a broad grin. "And I have a feeling we'll still see a lot of him."

Connie didn't respond as she passed on through the reception room and into her office. She tried to work, but couldn't keep her mind on the papers in front of her. Joseph didn't come for a half hour, and when he arrived, his forehead was wrinkled with perplexity and concern. He shut the door behind him.

Coming to Connie's desk, he reached in his pocket and handed her a newspaper clipping. She glanced quickly at the report of a pharmacy holdup, and a picture of two robbers looting the store, caught by a video camera.

"Rose found this in those papers she brought from my in-laws' house. She thinks the person on the left is Virginia."

"Your wife?" Connie looked at the picture again. "The images are fuzzy—it would be difficult to recognize anyone."

"That's true, but it could possibly be Virginia. A few people have hinted to me that she was wild and rebellious before I married her, and I know she was away from home for a year, and she wouldn't talk to me about what she did then.''

"If the robbery does concern Virginia, would it help your investigation?''

"Probably. If she had a criminal record, her death might be related to it, but I'll personally check it out before I give the information to my lawyers. I won't blacken Virginia's name without some proof she was involved in this robbery.''

Connie looked closely at the picture. "There isn't a date or any indication of where the robbery occurred.''

"No, and since the picture is blurred, I don't know how it's possible to know if one of the people is Virginia.''

Connie walked to the window and inspected the picture in natural light. "If this picture is enlarged, details in the background might provide a clue to where the robbery occurred. It looks like there's a name on the window. And you might try the Internet—there's information about *everything* there.''

"I'm not on the Internet. I wouldn't know how to go about it.''

"I'll do it, if you want me to,'' Connie said. "I could enlarge the picture to see if there's anything that will pinpoint the robbery, and then I could search on the Internet.''

"I'd appreciate it. I need all the help I can get. I'm desperate to prove I had nothing to do with my wife's death. Did you ever see that comic strip where a little guy had a black cloud hovering over his head all the time? That's the way I feel, as if a heavy cloud is floating over my head, ready to dump its contents on me.''

"If you talk to your brother-in-law, he might be able to tell you about this clipping."

"I haven't seen George since the time he accused me of taking Virginia's money—and killing her. I doubt he'd appreciate being asked if his sister was a criminal."

"Regardless, if we do learn anything that implicates Virginia, you should talk with him. If she had a shady past, he might know about it."

"That's true, for they were confidants and very close. That may have been the reason he introduced me to Virginia and encouraged our marriage—perhaps he thought I could save her from the mistakes of the past."

Connie went into the outer office, made an enlarged copy of the newspaper clipping, and returned the original to Joseph. He put the paper in his pocket and stood close to Connie.

"I can't tell you now how much you've meant to me in these few months. You've given me hope, as well as a desire to love again. I can hardly bear to leave you."

"I'll miss you, too, but we knew this day would come."

His hand caressed her hair. "After our little interlude on the mountain yesterday, do I still have to ask permission to kiss you?" Shaking her head, she put her hands on his shoulders.

His arms pulled her close, and his lips caressed hers. Trembling, she clung to him when the kiss ended, dreading seeing him go, but thankful that she'd been given the opportunity to know and learn to love Joseph. Knowing what real love was would fortify her for the ordeal she faced with Ray.

"I'll telephone you often," Joseph promised as he left.

Chapter Seven

Connie telephoned Ray on Friday evening and arranged an appointment at nine o'clock the next morning. Her sleep was restless, due partly to the approaching unpleasantness with Ray, but also because Joseph was no longer around. She was accustomed to his absence on weekends, but she knew she'd start looking for him on Monday morning.

When she joined Peggy for their early-morning run, the trails reminded her of Joseph and the time she'd spent with him. After her hurtful experience with Ray, she wasn't completely comfortable with the idea of marriage, so, even if he wanted to marry her, she wasn't ready to accept. Besides, she didn't believe he would consider marriage until the mystery of his wife's death was unraveled. She could understand why he felt that way, but nonetheless, she contemplated a bleak and lonely future. Did Joseph still love his wife? Connie suspected that he did, and that it would be a long time before Virginia's memory would give room for another woman in Joseph's life.

Ray and Eric were already in the office when Connie arrived. She sat behind her desk, hands clenched in her lap. When she spoke, her calm voice surprised her. It seemed a small miracle, considering her heart pounded like a jackhammer.

"I'm sure you're aware of why I called this meeting," Connie began, "for Laura would have reported to you immediately." Ray answered with a smirk. "Your moral principles are your own, and I can't dictate them. However, your behavior isn't in the best interests of my patients. I'm asking for your resignation."

Ray laughed loudly. "I didn't think you had the guts to fire me," he said. He reached in his pocket and pulled out an envelope. "I've waited a month to have you kick me out."

"If you felt that way, why didn't you resign?"

"I figured you'd sue me for breaking my contract, but since you've asked for my resignation, here it is. I already have an offer from a big gym in Denver. Suppose you'll have a hard time replacing me?"

In spite of his attempt to annoy her, Connie said sincerely, "You're a good therapist, and I wish you could stay, but under the circumstances, it won't work. If you didn't already have a job, I'd be happy to give you a recommendation. It's your moral character that I can't accept."

"You're a good one to talk about moral character, when you jumped from my arms into Joseph Caldwell's. You'd have come back to me if he hadn't shown up at NLC."

She shook her head. "No! Joseph had nothing to do with it."

Ray stood rapidly, and his chair fell backward. "We'll meet again, Connie. You might change your mind."

He walked out the door, and Connie's shoulders slumped as she turned to Eric.

"Do you suppose he'll continue to annoy me?"

"I'm afraid so, but I doubt he'll attempt to harm you. He's just angry."

"Now, the big job starts. Where will I find a new manager? I have to keep the gym open—it's one of the few programs around here that actually pays its way."

Joseph telephoned that night. Kim and Eric had gone into Denver for the evening, so Connie was alone in her apartment.

"This is Joseph," he said when she answered. "I've been anxious to know how you got along to-day."

"Well enough, I suppose. Ray's gone, and that gives me some relief. He could have stayed for two more months, but he's already gotten a job. I'll have to look for a new manager in the gym."

"Will that be a problem?"

"It won't be easy to replace him. In spite of his other faults, he is a good trainer, but Kim has advertised in town and on the Internet, and we're expecting to be barraged with applicants. Choosing one will be the problem."

"I'm missing you, Connie."

"Life has been rather dull around here today, too. But I've already been assigned a new patient."

"A female, I hope."

"No, as a matter of fact, he's a tall, handsome male with a charming personality."

Joseph groaned.

"And he's fifteen years old," she added.

A loud whoosh filled Connie's ear. "What a relief!"

"It's the Cartland boy who was hurt in a sports accident. He has quite a lot of nerve damage, so I don't know how much I can do for him."

"You'll do great—just think how much I improved. I'm looking forward to having you, Kim and Eric visit. Are you still planning on it?"

"As far as I know, unless something happens around here. I hope I'll have time before then to trace that picture on the Internet to find out the name and location of the publication."

"I've wondered if there aren't some clues here in the house. I haven't gone through Virginia's things, and I didn't want my sister to do it unless I was here. The police snooped around, and as far as I know they didn't find anything, but other than that, her room is just as she left it."

"We'll keep searching until we find something," Connie assured him. She wasn't keen about checking out Virginia's possessions, but it might come to that. She cared about Joseph, and she intended to fight to clear his name.

Joseph's call boosted Connie's spirits, and Ray's departure ended the tension she'd experienced since the broken engagement. His absence made life much easier for her, but she soon found Ray had made problems so she couldn't easily forget him. Two of the exercise machines, the double-arm bench press and the double-arm pull, broke down on Wednesday, and although there was no way she could prove it, she believed Ray had deliberately sabotaged the equipment. Repairing the machines would be expensive and the parts couldn't be delivered for two weeks, which meant a loss of income for Connie, as well as an inconvenience to her customers.

After worrying over the financial crisis these problems would generate, Connie was relieved to get away for a few days when they left NLC on Friday evening. Her parents had arrived shortly after noon and moved into the apartment she and Kim shared, and she wasn't concerned about leaving the property, for no trouble would escape Bill Harmon.

Joseph's directions were easy to follow and Eric's car covered the miles easily. In two hours, they drove through an open gateway with a stock barrier in the pavement. At the entrance, a large board shaped like an ox yoke and supported by two large cedar posts indicated they'd reached the right place. Flying Arrow Ranch, Joseph Caldwell, Owner, was painted on the sign.

Admiring the large white cattle grazing on knee-high wild hay, they drove for a mile on a limestone road before coming to the ranch buildings. A two-story buff brick house, facing south, nestled against a low hill that protected it from winter's northerly winds. Level plains surrounded the ranch to the east and north, but westward, majestic mountains loomed like guardians over Joseph's property.

A curved driveway brought them to the front of the house, and Joseph rose from a chair on the porch and hurried toward the car, followed by a tall brunette of regal bearing. Shaking hands with them, Joseph said, "This is my sister, Jean, she'll be my hostess for the weekend. She doesn't think I can entertain visitors without her help, and she's probably right. Jean has a ranch ten miles away, and she's been looking after my property for the past six months."

"Come in," Jean said. "We're pleased to have you visit. Joseph has nothing but praise for the staff at NLC, so I'm happy to finally meet you."

They entered a large room with a cathedral ceiling supported by round cedar beams, from which a brass chandelier, fashioned like a wagon wheel, was suspended on a long chain. A huge mural by a famous Western artist, featuring a roundup scene, hung over the stone-faced fireplace. Large andirons supported several logs in the fireplace, and beside it was a five-foot bronze sculpture of a cowboy riding a bucking bronco.

When Eric commented on the sculpture, Jean commented in an aside to Kim and Connie, "That was one of Virginia's romantic notions. She said the statue reminded her of Joseph when he rode in the state fairs. It might have been better for her if she hadn't bought it."

Kim and Connie glanced at each other curiously, but Joseph had joined them, and Jean said nothing more.

The room contained massive leather furniture, with a recliner chair placed prominently in front of a large-screen television. This was definitely a man's room.

Virginia must have loved Joseph very much, Connie thought, and designed this room for him. It was the kind any cowman would like. The knowledge brought no comfort to her heart.

Jean's next words confirmed that her surmise was true. "Virginia furnished this room to please Joseph. She preferred more feminine things, and the key to her personality is in her sitting room next door. Which," she said to Eric, "is where I've put you for the weekend. There's a comfortable sofa bed in the room, if you can overlook all the feminine furbelows."

"No problem for me," Eric said. "I'm sure I'll get used to feminine things before many more weeks."

Jean laughed heartily. "I'm sure you will. Joseph tells me that you and Kim are marrying soon."

Kim and Connie peeked into the room Eric would occupy, and Connie learned a bit about the character of Joseph's wife based on the pastel colors, lacy curtains, plush cushions, dainty furnishings and white carpet. The room seemed out of place in this ranch setting. Had Virginia been a misfit here, too?

"I would ask you to sit down, but you're probably tired of sitting after that two-hour drive, and besides, dinner will be ready in a half hour," Jean said, "so I'll show you to your rooms, and you can settle in. Kim, you and Connie will share a room, if that's all right."

"Eric and I will bring in the bags," Joseph said.

After seeing Virginia Caldwell's private sitting room, the presence of Joseph's wife was heavy on Connie's mind as she followed Jean and Kim upstairs and down a narrow hallway. Had Joseph built this home for his wife? Did he still love her? They passed a closed door adjacent to Joseph's room, and she wondered if that had been Virginia's room. In light of her attraction to Joseph, Connie felt like an intruder.

Connie and Kim's room was comfortably furnished with twin beds, racks for their luggage and an empty closet ready for garment bags. Short white draperies matched the brocade bedspreads. Jean pointed to an open, screened window. "There's no air-conditioning here, so I'll close these windows now and pull the blinds to keep out the heat. You can open the windows when you go to bed. We get a nice breeze from the mountains, and it cools down considerably at night. Your bathroom is at the end of the hall."

Jean appeared to be several years older than Joseph. She didn't wear a wedding band, and Connie couldn't remember Joseph ever commenting on her marital state.

"It's nice of you to look after us this weekend," Kim said.

Jean carelessly waved her hand. "No bother. I live alone in the house my grandfather built, so I enjoy having company. In this area, ranches are scattered far and wide, and we don't get together often." As she left the room, she said, "Come on down to the living quarters when you're ready. I have iced lemonade waiting for you."

After dinner, Joseph suggested a tour of the ranch buildings. When Kim volunteered to help with the dishes, Jean said, "Of course not. You're guests, and it won't take me long to fill the dishwasher. As soon as I have the kitchen in order, I'll go home and be back in time for breakfast.''

"Do you want to walk or ride on the tour?" Joseph asked. "There's an ATV handy," he added, smiling at Connie.

"Don't remind me of that!" she said.

"Let's walk," Kim said. "If I don't get some exercise, Connie will probably make me go jogging at daybreak in the morning."

"She'll have to go," Joseph said, "whether she wants to or not." He fixed a stern gaze on Connie. "You forced me to walk and run when I didn't want to, so be prepared to roll out of bed at six o'clock in the morning. I've laid out a two-mile running track around the corral fence."

"You shouldn't punish Eric and me just because Connie was a hard taskmaster," Kim said, her eyes bubbling with mirth. "I'm on a holiday, so none of this early stuff for me. What can we do along about midmorning?"

"We can go riding, if you like. I have lots of horses," Joseph said. "There's a nice place for a picnic about an hour's ride away."

"That will be far enough for me to ride," Eric said with a laugh. "Remember I'm a city boy from Louisiana. I know nothing about horses."

"You will after tomorrow," Joseph said. "I'll ask Jean to pack a lunch for us. And I promise you," he added with a sly grin at Connie, "the food will be full of calories, but I don't believe that will hurt you. Have you lost weight?"

"No, but if I looked peaked, it's because we've

had a rough week. Thanks for inviting us here—we all needed to be away from NLC for a few days.''

"Your folks are in charge, I suppose?"

"Yes, and they sent their greetings to you."

"How about explaining your ranch work to us," Eric said. "Kim and Connie may know more than I do, but I've never been on a ranch before."

"We run about five hundred Hereford cattle, and a few Charolais. You may have seen them in the fields as you drove in. We harvest about twenty thousand tons of prime grass and alfalfa and raise enough grain to feed the cattle and horses. Most of my cattle are in summer pasture. I rent about five thousand acres of rangeland in the mountain valleys, and we take the cattle up there each spring. The summer range is thirty miles away, and one of my workers and his wife stay up there all summer, living in a somewhat primitive log cabin, but they enjoy it. Someone goes up once a week to take their mail and food supplies."

"I didn't realize ranching was such hard work," Kim said.

"I have three hired hands, and during haying, or when we're rounding up or vaccinating cattle, we work twelve to fifteen hours a day. Summer is our busy season—that's the reason I fretted so because I had to be away this summer."

Still the therapist, Connie asked, "Does your injury give you any trouble when you ride?"

"I'm aware of it when I'm in the saddle for several hours, but I'm thankful it's no worse."

After they'd looked at the horses in the corral and inspected the farm buildings, which were neat and in good repair, Kim and Eric turned back toward the house. "I want to try out those rocking chairs on the back porch, Joseph," Eric said.

"Help yourself—the view is great from there." To Connie, Joseph said, "Shall we walk down to the lake? It's not as scenic as the one at NLC, but it's a peaceful spot."

After they'd walked for a few minutes, Joseph said, "How are you managing this week since Ray Blazer left you without any warning?"

"We have been shorthanded, but I've hired a retired gymnast from Denver to help out until we can find a replacement for Ray. For months, Ray has been belligerent and impudent, and his attitude kept me upset most of the time, so I'm relieved he's no longer in our employ." She withheld her suspicions that Ray had tampered with the equipment.

Eyeing her keenly, Joseph said, "No sadness then over what might have been?"

Meeting his gaze unflinchingly, she said, "Not at all. I don't like to be on the outs with anyone, but in this case, it's unavoidable. I don't suppose I'll ever see Ray again, and that will suit me."

Deeming it time to change the subject, Connie said, "I wanted a chance to talk to you privately. I've not had much luck tracing the newspaper clipping, but I studied the enlarged picture with a magnifying glass. There's a newspaper in a rack that is fairly plain, and I believe the date on it was six years ago. The lettering on the window is Taylor Pharmacy, but I don't know if Taylor is the name of the town or of the people who own the business."

"I've also been studying the enlarged copy you gave me, and the female robber is wearing a large turquoise necklace, identical to one Virginia had. If it's still in her jewelry box, that would be a definite clue to place her at the crime scene.''

"That would be valuable evidence. I'm checking out towns named Taylor, and if they have a newspaper, I'm contacting the paper, describing the clipping, asking for information. It's a slow process. There are many towns in this country named Taylor, or Taylorsville,'' Connie said with a sigh.

"If it's too time consuming for you, I'll go to my lawyers. Probably I should have anyway.''

"No. I want to help. It's just frustrating that I'm not accomplishing anything. Give me a few more weeks.''

After walking in silence for several minutes, Joseph said, musingly, "If that date is right, and Virginia was involved, the robbery occurred a year before our wedding.''

"How long did you know Virginia before you were married?''

"About six months. George and I had been friends in college, and I'd visited his home a couple of times, but Virginia hadn't been there. We kept in touch after college, and I was best man at his wedding. That's where I met Virginia.''

Joseph took Connie's hand, and his touch was warm and welcome. They reached the lake and paused to watch a great blue heron stretch his long neck and, with one quick movement, snatch a fish from the lake. Quacking incessantly, a pair of mallards and their half-grown ducklings headed toward the bank when Joseph dipped a plastic scoop in a covered bucket hanging on a post and scattered cracked corn on the ground. Connie and Joseph moved away when the flock hurried up the bank to eat. Several Charolais cattle lay in the lush grass surrounding the lake, contentedly chewing their cuds.

The setting was peaceful, but with Joseph's next words, Connie's enjoyment of the scene diminished. "Jean has been pestering me to donate Virginia's clothes to the local hospital's charity bazaar. I'd like to get them out of the house, but I don't want to dispose of them in this area. I wouldn't want to walk down the street of Fort Collins and meet someone wearing my wife's clothes. Do you know of anyplace around Denver to take them?"

Connie hadn't expected this visit to be a continual reminder of the presence of Joseph's wife, and every word about Virginia Caldwell pricked her heart, but she answered evenly, "My home church, the place where Mom and Dad attend, operates a clothes pantry for low-income families. They price the items at a reasonable rate, but if the person is destitute, or if they've lost all of their possessions in a disaster, there's no charge. They would make good use of her clothes."

"Can you check with Beverly? If it's all right, the next time I come to Lakewood, I'll have one of the workers' wives pack everything in boxes, and I'll deliver them to your parents' home, or to the church."

"When there's a mystery about Virginia's death, do you think it's wise to give away her wardrobe without checking for clues?"

"Probably not, but I can't do it."

"Then, I will. We can store them in an empty room at NLC, and I'll check through the items when I have time." What better way to face the memory of Virginia than to inspect her garments and discard them! "Since I didn't know Virginia, it won't be an emotional experience for me, as it would be for you or Jean. In fact, I'll volunteer to do the packing while we're here. I want to see your name cleared, Joseph, and we shouldn't overlook any possible clue."

"You're sure you don't mind?" he asked.

"Not at all—I'll do it after the picnic tomorrow." Connie knew it wasn't a Christian attitude, but, as much as she dreaded handling Virginia's possessions, she couldn't bear the thought of Joseph examining his wife's clothing and reminiscing about their lives together.

"It won't be an easy task. Virginia had lots of clothes. And I'll need to check the small safe where she kept her jewelry. It could hold a clue to help our search. The Perrys bought her many things, and she also inherited her mother's jewelry. I suppose I should give that to George—he has a daughter, and she should have her grandmother's jewels."

"That might be a good excuse for you to contact George and see what he knows. You could tell him you want to give Mrs. Perry's jewelry to his daughter, and while you're there, start questioning him."

"I don't know if I'm ready to talk to him yet." Joseph frowned, but then he laughed. "I guess I'll have to stop calling you 'Doc,' and start thinking of you as Sherlock Holmes. You'd make a first-rate detective."

"You were the one who suggested I might help you."

He put his arms around her shoulders and kissed

her lightly. "And I appreciate it, too. There aren't many people I'd trust with the information."

After his guests went to their rooms for the night, Joseph sat on the porch, deep in thought. One reason he'd invited Connie to the ranch was to see her in his home. Virginia had never liked the ranch. He'd built the house to please her, and she'd been intrigued at first at the opportunity to decorate the house to her own tastes, but it had never been home to her.

Virginia hadn't learned to ride. She'd thought horses smelled, and she hadn't liked feeling their sweaty hides on her legs. Before they were married, he'd anticipated that the two of them could spend long weekends in the cabin at the summer pasture, but Virginia had gone with him once to the area and dubbed the cabin a "primitive shack." Her idea of a weekend getaway was to Palm Springs, a Caribbean cruise or to Las Vegas. After a year, Joseph admitted to himself that he'd made a mistake, but he didn't complain to anyone. He'd married until "death do us part," and he lived with his mistake.

But he couldn't make another mistake! If he married again, he wanted a partner, someone to share his life. Connie had seemed to enjoy the ranch tonight, and she'd asked lots of questions about his methods of operation. Still, she had her own profession, and that was a two-hour drive away. If it was a nine to five job, she could commute back and forth to the ranch, but as director of NLC, she was on call most of the time. He couldn't ask her to give up her life's dream to marry him. Even if he was exonerated in

Virginia's death, he couldn't see any future with Connie.

Discouraged, he didn't go to his room until long after midnight. He changed into his sleeping shorts and looked for a long time at the closed door between his room and Virginia's. He hadn't opened it since Virginia's death. Joseph walked slowly toward the door, where he grasped the knob with a trembling hand. As he hesitated, sweat broke out on his forehead, and he turned away.

Determined to overcome his fear of the past, he approached the adjoining room quickly and forcefully opened the door, and experienced again the pain of losing Virginia forever. The room was ready for her— just as it had been nine months ago. Before she'd left the house for the day, the maid had turned down the heavy comforter, and the pink silk sheets and pillowcases were ready for Virginia's rest. A white nightgown and matching robe lay across the foot of the bed. His wife's cosmetics were laid out on the vanity dresser.

He went to the wall safe and opened a chest that contained her Native American jewelry and found the turquoise necklace. He no longer doubted Virginia's guilt, and he closed the safe and spun the combination. He walked slowly around the room, remembering the pleasures and the problems his marriage had brought. He paused in the doorway, and quietly said, "Goodbye, Virginia," before he returned to his room.

Joseph awakened at five o'clock, as was his custom during the summer months. Should he disturb Connie's sleep? He was half joking when he'd threatened her with an early-morning run, but it might be a good idea. He changed into shorts and a sweatshirt, walked down the hall and tapped lightly on the door where Kim and Connie slept. He tapped a second time, and received a sleepy reply, "Yes?" He thought it was Connie's voice.

He cracked the door. "Connie, I'm going for a run. Do you want to go with me?"

"Yes," she whispered. "Give me a few minutes, and I'll meet you downstairs."

While he waited for her, Joseph went to the kitchen and poured two small glasses of orange juice. He was sipping on his when Connie hustled down the stairs, wearing a pair of gray sweatpants and a matching shirt. He handed her a glass of juice.

"That was quick," he said as she drank.

"I laid out my clothes last night, so it didn't take long."

"Kim still asleep?"

"Yes. She stirred a little, but she wants to rest. We'll be busy next week getting ready for her wedding."

They walked toward the corral, hand in hand.

"Oh, I hear a meadowlark," Connie cried. "We never hear them at the Center." They stopped, and located the large bird with a black V on its yellow breast, perched on the corral fence. They were close enough to see its pulsating throat as the bird bubbled with song. "What a way to start the morning!" She laughed. "It sounds to me as if he's saying, 'Fill up the teakettle.'"

"My mother was born near Litchfield, Nebraska,

and she always said the meadowlark's song was, 'Used to live in Litchfield.'"

"Whatever he's saying, it's a beautiful song."

A four-foot strip had been mown along the periphery of the corral fence. "I've only run on this a couple of times, and it may be a little rough, so be careful. When I mowed this path, I didn't anticipate having company when I jogged, so it may not be wide enough for the two of us to run abreast."

"You start out, and I'll keep a few feet behind you," Connie said.

Joseph's thigh and leg had healed, but for the first quarter mile, his leg was stiff and painful, and he ran slowly, but when his leg muscles warmed up, he increased speed and ran smoothly. As they passed the lake, they disturbed flocks of red-winged blackbirds which flew out of the cattails, noisily scolding the runners.

When they reached the halfway mark, Joseph glanced quickly over his shoulder, and Connie flashed him a smile. The trail widened, and she sped up to run beside him. His heart warmed to hear her steps pounding in unison with his. Was this what marriage to her would mean? Could they travel through life side by side sharing their dreams and spiritual commitments?

"I'm proud of you, Joseph." Connie panted as she halted for breath at the end of the path. "You're not a bit awkward, and your injury can't be detected at all when you run. Three months has made a lot of difference."

In more ways than one, Joseph thought as he watched Connie wipe perspiration from her glowing face and sit on the ground to go through a series of leg exercises. He couldn't imagine a life without Connie, and he'd only known her a few months. Six months after he'd met Virginia, they'd been married. Should he be more cautious this time?

Chapter Eight

"**D**o we look like cowhands or what?" Kim joked as they walked toward the corral. They'd brought jeans and plaid shirts with them, but Joseph had provided wide-brimmed hats from the hall closet. Connie suspected that she and Kim had been given headgear that had belonged to Virginia, and the hat felt weighty on her head.

"Move them dogies out," Eric responded loudly, and all of them laughed, for levity seemed out of place in his quiet character. The day started off in this carefree way, a break from routine that all of them needed.

Four horses were saddled when Joseph and his three guests arrived at the corral. "My favorite mount is a quarter horse," Joseph explained, as he put an affectionate arm around a sturdy brown gelding.

A short, wiry man held the reins of the other horses, and Joseph introduced him, "This is Danny

Keller. He's the ranch foreman, and he's carried the majority of the responsibility around here this year.''

Danny doffed his hat and greeted them with a toothy grin.

''Since you aren't experienced riders, I asked Danny to saddle these Morgan horses for you. They're easy-gaited and old enough that they won't be frisky.''

''Are you sure?'' Kim said, as she and Eric warily eyed the sleek brown horses, with dark manes and tails. Connie thought they looked docile enough. She hadn't been on a horse for several years, but she was eager to take the ride, for she wanted to see Joseph's ranch.

When Joseph helped her into the saddle, it seemed like a long way to the ground, and Connie was dizzy at first, but Joseph advised, ''Learn to trust your horse. Piaute knows her way around the ranch and won't need much help from you. Just hold the reins, and she'll follow my mount.''

''Why the name Piaute?''

''I bought several horses from a Native American, and gave them Indian names.''

With some effort, Joseph and Danny settled Kim and Eric into their saddles and adjusted their stirrups. Then, with one fluid movement, Joseph swung into his saddle. While admiring his skill, Connie wondered if he'd ever participate in another rodeo. If she were asked, she'd advise against it. Even if Joseph's hip had healed, bouncing up and down atop a twisting bronco wouldn't do it any good. At this point, however, she wasn't in a position to advise Joseph. Would she ever be?

Joseph took the lead, and Piaute moved out behind him with no guidance from Connie. Joseph followed a trail along a slow-moving creek that would eventually mingle its waters with the South Platte. Connie patted the smooth brown shoulder of the horse that provided her with a comfortable ride. The narrow trail made it necessary to ride single file, and she looked over her shoulder occasionally to see that Kim and Eric were following along.

Once she overcame her apprehension of riding, Connie watched for wildlife. A doe and her fawn grazed near the creek, but the doe hurriedly took her offspring into heavy foliage, where, with her ears pointed like antennae, she watched the riders. Somewhat familiar with Colorado animals, Connie recognized several brownish-gray spruce squirrels jumping from tree to tree, busily extracting seeds from evergreen cones. Small, striped chipmunks scattered before the horses, their cheeks bulging with food they'd scavenged from the ground. Striking jays, with gray, white and black plumage, noisily protested the human invasion. She saw no beaver, but several fallen logs indicated that this stream provided a habitat for them.

When the trail became steeper, Connie felt added pressure on her back and thighs, and by the time Joseph halted his horse on the shore of a small lake, one of her legs prickled with little spurts of pain, and the other one was partially numb. She was ready to dismount when Joseph swung easily from the saddle and came to her side.

"Will this site be okay for a picnic?"

Water gushed from the lake into a narrow chute, tumbling noisily over a rocky base to form a tiny cataract. Douglas firs dotted the foothills, some of them bent and distorted from natural disasters. A maple tree hung over a wide, flat rock near the lake, providing a canopy for their picnic. With his guests displaying saddle weariness, Joseph said, "Walk around and get the stiffness out of your joints while I start a fire and prepare our lunch." When Kim and Connie protested, he added, "You're my guests today. I don't need any help."

When they returned a half hour later, the fire had dwindled to a glowing bed of coals, and four steaks sizzled on a small, portable grill. Ears of corn, wrapped in foil, lay at the edge of the coals, and Joseph used tongs to turn them. He'd spread a blanket on the big rock, and had set out a thermos of decaf, a bowl of fruit salad, brown bread, bottles of pink grapefruit punch and a peach pie.

"I suppose you prepared all of this food," Kim said pertly to Joseph.

"No, I can't take much credit—all I'm doing is grilling the steaks. Jean fixed everything else."

The aroma of the sizzling steaks tantalized Connie's taste buds, and she passed around the plates, waiting for the tasty steaks to be ready. She requested her meat well-done, while the others preferred medium-rare, so she had to wait longer for her portion. When she finally sank her teeth into the succulent beef, she said, "Oh, this is tasty!"

The others only mumbled a reply—they were too busy eating to talk.

"This is a great experience for me," Eric said. "Thanks for inviting us, Joseph. Our leisure time is a lot different in Louisiana. No mountains there, but we lived near the river, so we did a lot of fishing and boating, and we had fried fish on our outings rather than grilled steak. My parents taught me to water-ski when I was a child. I miss that.''

"There's waterskiing on some of our lakes. You'll have to check that out," Joseph said.

Kim and Eric helped pack the lunch utensils before they wandered away, hand in hand. Connie and Joseph sat silently for several minutes, and she knew he was uncomfortable because he squirmed on the hard rock. His face had lost much of the animation he'd displayed earlier in the day, and he stared blankly across the smooth blue waters of the lake that reflected the large stand of firs on the opposite bank.

"Penny for your thoughts," Connie said, smiling at him.

He leaned back against the maple tree and reached for Connie's hand. She moved closer to him, and he put an arm around her shoulders, and even that mere contact brought a ripple of pleasure. How much longer would she be content to be Joseph's friend? She liked his brotherly touches, and she had no one to blame except herself that he'd limited his more emotional caresses.

"I doubt they're worth a penny, but I can't stop thinking about the events leading up to Virginia's death. During the months I concentrated on recovering, I deliberately avoided thinking about that mystery, but now that we've started looking into the matter, it's constantly on my mind."

"Joseph, I don't like to dwell on what-ifs, but the more I try to learn something, the more I realize that there are very few clues to follow. How long do you expect to search? What will happen if you can't prove anything at all?"

He shook his head. "It won't surprise me if the police decide to arrest me on suspicion. They may have been biding their time until I was out of rehab. If I'm taken before a jury without any more proof than I have, I could be found guilty and possibly be sent to prison."

"Joseph!"

"It's scary, isn't it? I probably wouldn't be housed with hardened criminals, perhaps I'd be put in a medium-security prison. But even that would be terrible, especially when I haven't done anything wrong."

Joseph behind bars where he couldn't enjoy the freedom of riding the range! Connie had to fight off a feeling of hatred for the Perrys whose actions had put this man under suspicion—Virginia, who'd written the incriminating letter, and George, who'd believed she was writing about Joseph.

"Then we must work even harder to prove your innocence. There has to be evidence somewhere."

Joseph tugged gently on her hair and leaned over to plant a kiss on her cheek. "Thanks for being on my side."

"I'm not the only One. Remember the promise that 'if God is for us, who can be against us.' You aren't the first of His followers who've been brought before magistrates."

"That's true, but I also know that some of those followers have been thrown to the lions. I'm no better than the early Christian martyrs, so I'll have to take what comes."

Connie gently swatted his arm. "Stop those gloomy thoughts! Be more optimistic!"

"I'll try," he said penitently. "But it's easy to be pessimistic when your life is on hold. I can't make any plans until I know what my immediate future holds. You understand that, don't you?"

She assumed he meant future plans concerning *her*. "I'm not sure I do understand your attitude about the future. The future is always uncertain—we never know what tomorrow will bring."

He grinned. "Dad used to say the only thing certain about the future is death and taxes."

"Death is *not* uncertain when you're ready to go to Heaven and spend eternity with God!"

"I know," Joseph agreed. "I spoke about earthly things." He squirmed uncomfortably, and continued, "My leg has had enough of this hard rock," and he stood, pulling Connie up beside him and into his arms. She lifted a hand, and her fingers pulled gently at his ear, and traced the outline of his cheeks and mouth. Joseph caught her hand and nibbled on her fingers. Their kiss was long, and they didn't break the embrace until they heard Kim and Eric returning.

Although Joseph was aware that Connie was now more than willing to accept his caresses, he exercised restraint in their physical encounters. He wouldn't promise Connie more than he was able to give. Her reactions to the ranch had been positive, and he believed she could easily fit into his rural lifestyle, but until he was able to prove his innocence, he wouldn't make any move to further their romance. Always when he thought of marrying Connie, he remembered Virginia, their storybook wedding and first year of marriage. Would a union with her also grow sour, or would theirs last forever? As hard as it was to appear indifferent to the possibility of the love she could offer, he couldn't speak his mind.

Their conversation further convinced Connie that unless Joseph could be completely exonerated in the events surrounding the death of his wife, there was no future for the two of them. And the more she looked into the situation, the more she concluded that it was unlikely that Joseph could be freed from suspicion. So should she just stop longing for Joseph? Rationally thinking, that seemed the right thing to do, but she found it difficult to think sanely when she was dealing with her heart. And she couldn't help wonder if Joseph's hesitance didn't stem from his memories of Virginia, rather than from the crime hanging over his head.

Kim and Jean insisted that they'd help pack Virginia's clothes, so that evening, while Eric and Joseph watched a golf match on television, the three women went into Virginia's room and started the grim task. While the others had been picnicking, Jean had gone into town and purchased a large supply of cartons. A hint of oriental fragrance permeated the room as they worked.

In a low voice, Jean said, "I can't tell you what a relief it is to get these items out of the house. I wanted to do it before Joseph was released from the hospital, but he objected. I feared he'd make a shrine out of this room and would never change it."

"Did he love Virginia deeply?" Kim asked, and

Connie was sure her friend had posed the question because she thought Connie wanted to know.

"Yes, he did," Jean said, "and I've never understood why. Virginia was the clinging-vine type, and they were mismatched. She'd hated the ranch, but at least Joseph had enough backbone not to sell out and move into town as she wanted to."

"Do you have any idea what happened here the night she died?" Connie asked.

"Virginia must have been drunk, lost her balance, fallen, and hit her head on that bronze sculpture by the fireplace in the main room. Whether that caused her death, I haven't a clue, but it could have happened that way."

"When did she start drinking?"

"Before she met Joseph, I'm sure, and she must have hid the habit from him, or he wouldn't have married her, unless he thought he could reform her. After three years of marriage, she left him, and I figured he would divorce her then, but she asked to come back, so he let her."

Taking a short mink coat from its wrapping, Connie said, "I told Joseph that I'd take these clothes to our church for resale to needy families—such nice garments will be greatly appreciated, I'm sure."

"I wanted to take them to the charity bazaar at the local hospital," Jean said, "but Joseph didn't want them sold locally." Running her fingers over the smooth fur of the coat, Jean continued, "Joseph didn't have the money to buy clothes like these, but Virginia's father still gave her a monthly allowance even after they were married, and she'd go to New York on a spending spree every year. Virginia might have been more satisfied here if she would have lived on Joseph's income.'' She shrugged her shoulders. ''But all that's in the past. I'm not one to dwell on what might have been.''

Is Joseph longing for the past and what might have been? Connie wondered, but her heart didn't really want to know.

''Most of these are winter clothing,'' Kim said as she held up a red woolen suit. ''Did she have other clothes?''

''Of course she did! I hadn't thought of that,'' Jean said. ''She didn't have enough space in her closets, so Virginia kept seasonal items in her room and stored the others in the attic. They'll be packed in bags or chests, so I'll send them along, too.''

They left the ranch Sunday in midafternoon with promises from Joseph and Jean to be at NLC in two weeks for the wedding of Kim and Eric.

Two weeks! Connie thought that was a long time not to see Joseph, and he must have thought so, too, for the next Thursday, he appeared at her office door about noon.

''Hello!'' she said. ''What brings you our way?''

''I had a business meeting in Denver, and I brought those cartons of clothing along. It didn't seem appropriate to bring them on Kim's wedding day.''

''You're right,'' she said. Connie closed the client's progress file she'd been reviewing and put it in a desk drawer. ''If you'll bring your truck to the rear door of this building, I'll help you carry the boxes into a storeroom.''

"Have you made any progress with your detective work?"

"Very little. I've sent queries to a dozen newspapers, asking them to search their files, and I printed the caption under the picture, hoping someone will remember the incident. I offered a reward of fifty dollars to anyone who sends any information. Nothing, so far, but I'll keep searching. The key to the mystery may be in that photo."

"Keep track of any expense you have, and I'll pay it."

"There's been no expense yet."

It was almost time for lunch when they had the boxes unloaded, and Connie suggested, "Why not have lunch with us? The staff and patients will be happy to see you."

"Thanks," he drawled. "I hoped you'd ask. I want to talk to Rose, anyway."

Connie and Joseph lingered in the cafeteria until everyone left, and Connie asked Rose to sit in on a conference with them. They chose a table in the corner farthest from the kitchen so they wouldn't be overheard.

"Rose," Joseph started, "I had nothing to do with the death of my wife, and now that I'm on my feet again, I'm trying to prove it. The police are so convinced that I'm implicated that they've stopped looking any further. Connie has agreed to help me, and I hope I can count on you."

"Lands, Mr. Caldwell, it never occurred to me that you were responsible," Rose said, laying a plump hand on his shoulder. "But I don't know what I can do."

"You've already helped by producing that newspaper clipping. Do you have any idea where you got it?"

Rose shook her head. "I don't remember seeing it until a couple of weeks ago when I was looking for that pie recipe. You see, a few months after Mr. Perry died, George and his wife, Stephanie, moved into the house. She wanted to bring the household staff from her own home, so there was no place for me, but George told me to take anything from the kitchen I wanted to. I'm a great one to cut recipes out of magazines, and I had a basket full of them in my room. I put all of the clippings in a box, intending to sort them out when I got the time. Maybe when I was cutting out a recipe, that clipping fell into the basket, but I don't know."

"There isn't a recipe on the back of it," Connie said, "for I checked that right away. The other side had nothing on it to pinpoint the date or the location of the newspaper."

"Would anyone else have had access to the basket where you kept the recipes?" Joseph asked.

"I kept the basket on a shelf in the kitchen. Anyone could have found it if they wanted to."

"Did Mrs. Perry sometimes bring you recipes—suggestions of what she wanted you to prepare?" Connie asked.

Rose's eyes brightened. "No, but Virginia did. That time she left you and came home for several months, Mr. Caldwell, she considered herself the lady of the house, and quite often she'd study gourmet magazines and bring me a menu she wanted served when she entertained her friends."

"So, it's possible that clipping could have been in some recipes she brought you," Connie said.

"I suppose so."

"Now, Rose, what can you tell me about Virginia before I met her? I visited the Perry home two different weekends the last year I was at the university, and Virginia wasn't at home either time. Where was she?"

Rose fidgeted in her chair and wouldn't meet Joseph's gaze. "I don't like to speak ill of the dead."

"Any information you have isn't going to hurt Virginia, but it might do Joseph a lot of good," Connie insisted.

"Actually, I don't know where she was, and her parents didn't know, either. She and one of her girlfriends were supposedly taking a tour of the United States. She telephoned her mother a few times, and when the Perrys received statements of credit card withdrawals, they assumed she was all right, but if they knew where she was, they didn't say." She laughed. "In big houses like that, there's usually an unspoken conspiracy among the staff to find out what their employers are doing. So I don't think any of the servants knew where Virginia was. It worried me, too, for I was fond of the girl, and I didn't think her mother gave her enough supervision."

"Didn't you know anything about this, Joseph?" Connie asked.

He shook his head. "Virginia often mentioned places in the United States and overseas where she'd traveled, but I assumed it was in the company of her family. I must be the most naive person in the world," he added in disgust. "Virginia was all right when I met her, and I didn't pry into her past."

"I don't know any particulars, but after several months," Rose continued, "the news circulated that Virginia was in the hospital and her father and George went someplace and brought her home, but I didn't know where she'd been hospitalized. Two nurses came to the house and cared for her several months, but the household staff wasn't given any information about what was wrong with her, we figured she must have been in a detox hospital for drug addicts."

Joseph's face blanched, and he moaned, "Surely not!"

"I think so," Rose said. "Even as a high school student, she'd held a few parties when her parents were away, and the servants knew they were up to something. But after she came back home, as far as I know, she went straight, for her parents guarded her carefully until you married her."

"If George was the kind of friend he should be, he would've told me all of that."

"He probably figured you wouldn't marry her if you knew how wild she'd been," Rose answered. "Mr. Perry was desperate to get Virginia married to a decent man, and you were the answer to their problem."

"The whole family did court me," Joseph said grimly. "I wasn't in their social class, and it surprised me that they approved of our marriage. Now I learn that they were only using me. I would have married her even if they'd told me, but either Virginia or her family should have leveled with me. George plotted against me even before he accused me of killing his sister!''

Obviously, this further disloyalty on the part of a friend he'd trusted had depressed Joseph, and Connie attempted to refocus his attention on his current need. ''It's apparent that the clue to Virginia's death lies in that year she was away from home. Do either of you know the name of the friend who was with her during that year?''

''Her name was Debbie Smith then, but she's married now,'' Rose answered.

''I know Debbie,'' Joseph said. ''She was Virginia's maid of honor, and she came to the ranch quite often until she took a job in California and married someone out there. I believe she's divorced now and has returned to Colorado. Her father used to manage a motel north of Denver. I can probably get a lead on Debbie by telephoning the motel.''

Joseph stood and shook Rose's hand. ''You've been quite helpful, Rose, and I appreciate it. Let Connie know if you think of anything else that seems pertinent. I'm praying for peace of mind, and the strength to forgive George, but I'll never be free of the past until I find out what really happened.''

Connie was scheduled to meet Tom Cartland for a therapy session, but she took time to walk with Joseph to his truck.

''Where do we go from here?'' she asked.

''Although I dread it, I'm going to contact George, and after I find out what he knows, I'll get in touch with Debbie. I'd rather not face him alone, and Jean would jump at the chance to go, but she's too outspoken, and would be pleased to give George a tongue-lashing. I hesitate to ask this, but will you go with me when I visit George? It will be easier for me.''

"I want to go, if you can arrange the visit when it won't interfere with my work schedule—a Saturday or Sunday afternoon would be best, but not until after the wedding. Kim and I are making floral arrangements and favors for the reception, and until the wedding is over, I won't even have time to go through Virginia's possessions to see what I can find.''

Since they had met at NLC, Kim and Eric wanted to be married there. The chapel was too small for the guests they invited, so Kim and Connie planned a wedding on the lawn behind the administration building. They'd chosen the first Sunday in August, hoping for a shower-free afternoon. Kim's parents were close friends of Bill and Beverly Harmon, and the four of them spent hours at NLC transforming the lawn into a wedding bower. The couple would take their vows in a white gazebo with an arched entrance, covered with live greenery from the mountains, interspersed with white silk daisies.

Eric and Kim planned a short, simple ceremony, and they'd written their own vows based on the Scripture, ''Your body is a temple of the Holy Spirit, who is in you, whom you have received from God. You are not your own; you were bought at a price. Therefore honor God with your body.'' Their devotion to the Marriage First conviction was indicated in these vows.

Wedding guests included only family and close friends, but Kim's family was large and twenty of

Eric's family came from Louisiana. Eric's brother and Connie were the only attendants, and the pastor of Kim's church in Lakewood performed the ceremony.

Still hurting over the rift in her Marriage First group caused by the deviousness of Laura and Ray, Connie was heartened by the pure wedding of Kim and Eric. They wore the Marriage First pins on their wedding day.

Joseph and Jean came to the wedding, and when the bride and bridegroom took their vows, Connie sensed Joseph looking at her, and she met his solemn gaze. How she wished she knew what he was thinking! Perhaps he looked forward to a day when they would be married, or more likely, he remembered the day he'd married Virginia. During the reception, Joseph shook hands with Eric, kissed Kim on the cheek, but only patted Connie's hand. "Bridesmaids don't get kissed at a wedding," he said, "and especially not without an invitation."

She grimaced at him as he moved on.

Since NLC had been responsible for her brother's recovery, Jean was interested in the facility and asked for a tour. She was so impressed by their program that she gave Connie a check for five hundred dollars. "You're doing wonderful work here, Connie—use this little contribution where you need it."

Connie was touched. "We have plenty of places to use your gift," she told Jean, "but I'll wait until Kim returns from her honeymoon before I spend it, since she keeps track of NLC's finances."

Chapter Nine

During the week Kim and Eric were away on their honeymoon, Connie spent every night sifting through Virginia's possessions. It was a heartrending time for her as she handled the designer clothing that Virginia had worn. A haunting combination of jasmine, musk and lily of the valley permeated all the boxes, and Connie knew she would never again smell this shimmering oriental fragrance without thinking of Virginia. Did Joseph associate that scent with Virginia? Did he still love his wife? Even if they solved the mystery of Virginia's death, would he ever marry again?

After the first evening of riffling through Virginia's belongings, Connie was so agitated that she contemplated hauling the boxes to the clothes pantry without looking at the rest of them. After she'd worked in the storeroom for several hours, Connie couldn't sleep when she went to bed later on. Even in death, Virginia Caldwell stood between her and Joseph. Connie tried to develop an idea of Virginia's personality as she assessed the clothing the woman had worn. The garments all contained exclusive designer labels, and Connie couldn't imagine anyone having so many clothes. Numerous items had never been taken from the wrappers. Many of her garments were made of lightweight fabrics in pastel shades, and Connie envisioned Virginia as a pampered woman, spoiled by her parents and perhaps Joseph, too, although from what Jean had said, he wouldn't have had the money to provide the clothing. Connie pegged her as a selfish, indecisive person, one who avoided responsibility. But in all fairness, she admitted that she probably *wanted* to characterize Virginia as that type of person. Based on the same facts, Joseph's wife could just as easily have been quiet, easy to get along with and full of compassion and concern.

Yet these assumptions might all be wrong, for Connie had never even seen a picture of the woman who occupied her thoughts. At the ranch, she'd expected to see a portrait of Virginia, but if there had ever been any photos of her, they'd been removed. After each restless night of looking through her things, Connie realized how foolish she was to be intimidated by a dead woman, so she determined that, in spite of the emotional stress, she'd finish what she'd started.

By Wednesday evening, Connie had looked through half of the boxes without finding any evidence that would lead to Joseph's vindication. The next night she checked the cartons that had been stored in the attic at the ranch house—items that looked as if they hadn't been used for many years. In the bottom of one box, she found Joseph and Virginia's wedding album, which upset her emotional equilibrium for weeks after.

Virginia Caldwell had been beautiful, and on her wedding day, she'd glowed with happiness. In one picture, she gazed up at Joseph as if she couldn't believe her good fortune in having him for a husband. A petite blonde, with vivid green eyes set in a peach blossom complexion, Virginia's head was on a level with Joseph's shoulders. Everything about Virginia—clothing, physical structure, and poise—proclaimed her femininity.

Her exquisite, ostentatious gown, which must have cost thousands, was enhanced by a floor-length veil that flowed backward from a golden crown, and a long train that spread gracefully over the steps leading to the chancel of the church. Every aspect of the wedding and reception spoke of wealth.

And Joseph? There was no doubt that he was happy, too, and how long would it take to get over losing someone you loved as much as he must have loved his wife? Looking at his youthful countenance five years ago, it was evident that the past months of illness, and being a suspect in his wife's death, had taken their toll on him. Connie couldn't bear to look at the pictures, and she put the album back in the box.

Still holding it, she plopped down on the floor of the storeroom comparing herself to Virginia, and accepting an unpleasant reality. Joseph had chosen Virginia, so she thought it was doubtful that he could ever generate a romantic interest in her. She'd never been uncomfortable with her own physical characteristics, but now she conceded that she came in a poor second place when compared to Virginia. A tall, lanky, tomboyish physical therapist wouldn't appeal to a man who'd been married to a woman possessing all the elegance and refinement that wealth could bring.

So then, where did that leave her association with Joseph? Did his pleasure in her company stem from the therapist-patient association they'd had? That must be it, for Joseph had insisted that he hadn't considered a premarital relationship with her, and she believed him. After almost daily companionship for three months, he would naturally feel some closeness to her—perhaps it was more of a brotherly emotion, but whatever it was, Connie knew it wouldn't be enough for her. She'd committed to helping him solve the mystery of Virginia's death, and she'd do that, but when his name was cleared, what then? Joseph would be able to go on with his life, and somehow she'd make it easy for him to go on without her.

Connie didn't like that solution, but she didn't know what else she could do. After the altercation when she'd thought Joseph had propositioned her, he'd promised that he wouldn't kiss her again until she was ready. To her shame, she remembered that on Faith Mountain she'd been the first to break the agreement by kissing him. He'd kissed her when he left NLC, but would he have done so if she hadn't been so obvious in her feelings for him?

Connie got up from the floor, knowing that if she kept stewing about the past, she'd soon be wallowing in self-pity, and she had no patience with that attitude. What should she do with the photo album? Obviously she couldn't send it to the church. Before she put the lid on the box, she glanced at some loose photos lying beneath the album. Most of the pictures were of Virginia, and presumably George, when they were children, but one was of three adults. It was a beach picture with Virginia and another young woman, scantily clad, standing on either side of a barefoot, bearded man wearing jean cutoffs and sandals. "San Diego," and a date, was scrawled on the back, and judging by the date, the picture could have been taken during the year Virginia had been absent from her home. It could mean something or it might not, but Connie laid it aside to show Joseph.

Other than the picture, the week of searching produced nothing that would exonerate Joseph, but it left Connie with anguish she figured time would never erase. Probably she'd learned nothing that would help the man she loved, and she'd experienced enough heartache to last for a lifetime. The next day, the gardener helped her load the boxes in the van, and she took them to the church in Lakewood. All trace of Virginia Caldwell had been removed from the ranch house and the storeroom at NLC. How Connie wished she could so easily erase memories of the woman from her mind—and Joseph's.

Connie telephoned Joseph Saturday evening.

"Hi," she said when he answered. "I've checked through all of those cartons, without much success. I do have a picture of Virginia, another woman and a man, which may have been taken in San Diego during the year she was gone. Outside of that, I found nothing suspicious, and I haven't had any response from any of the newspapers I've contacted. The first of the week, I'll start checking out San Diego newspapers."

"I struck out on my first attempt to see George, too. When I telephoned his office, I learned he'll be gone for another week."

"Next Monday is when we have our wagon train trip into the forest. Are you still planning to go with us, Joseph?"

"As far as I know."

"Then meet us at the first picnic area inside Roosevelt National Forest next Monday at ten o'clock."

"How many are going?"

"Twenty, plus the workers the outfitter will bring."

"I'll provide my own horse and equipment. I prefer a familiar mount and saddle."

"I'm pleased you're going, Joseph, and I hope you enjoy the week."

Bill and Beverly always supervised the grounds of NLC while the others enjoyed a holiday. It was a time of relaxation for them too, for in the absence of staff and patients, Bill spent the time fishing, and Beverly walked the easy trails and spent a lot of time in the pool. The gates were closed and locked, so not even any curious passersby could disturb them.

Connie enjoyed the trail ride, and she was looking forward to it even more this year because Joseph was going along. Kim and Eric rode to the rendezvous with Connie, who had the rear of the van piled high with food supplies. Rose was going along as cook, and she'd helped Connie choose menus that required a lot of groceries. Appetites usually tripled in the great outdoors!

Della Sinnet rode with Rose in her car, for the wagon train was the high point of her summer before she headed for a warmer climate. Some of the participants had gone each of the three years, and even though they no longer needed the services of NLC, they liked the camaraderie of the trail, so the wagon trip was also a reunion for some NLC graduates.

Five wagons were lined up near the entrance when Connie drove into the campground. These wagons were much larger than the covered wagons of the past. They had benches on each side for seating, and the canvas rolled up to afford a good view for those who rode in the wagon. A couple of people could spread out their bedrolls on the floor at night, but most participants preferred to sleep in small tents. Always before, Connie and Kim had bunked together, but since Kim and Eric would share a tent this trip, Connie elected to sleep alone.

Connie made it a point to arrive well before her guests. She wanted to be on hand to greet them—it was uplifting for her to be reunited with patients whom NLC had been able to help. Joseph came soon after the three of them arrived, accompanied by his foreman, Danny Keller, and pulling a stock trailer behind his pickup. Smiling, Joseph waved to them, and when he stepped jauntily from the truck, Connie remembered the pain he'd been in, and how he'd limped when she'd first met him. She recalled the first week when he struggled to walk a few yards. As he smilingly came to greet her, she thanked God again for guiding her into the field of physical and spiritual therapy. This was the first time Connie had seen him since she'd deduced so much about his wife's character, but she was determined that Joseph would never know how she'd been humbled by her own comparison of herself to Virginia.

"Hello," she said, and Joseph took her hand.

"I brought my own horse and gear, and also the mare you rode at the ranch when you visited. You seemed to like her."

Connie ran to the stock trailer and reached a hand through the opening to pat the sleek flank of the horse.

"Hi, Piaute," she said. "Thanks, Joseph. As you know, I'm not a skilled rider, and it will be better for me to have a familiar mount."

Eric and Kim joined them. "How's everything at the ranch?" Eric said.

"Going smoothly right now, but I do feel a bit guilty going off and leaving the men with all the work after I've been away for so many months."

"You need a vacation like the rest of us. They'll manage," Kim said.

Joseph patted his pocket. "I did bring my cell phone, so they can reach me in an emergency. How did you honeymooners like your trip to Los Angeles?"

"Different from Colorado, but neither of us had ever been there, so we enjoyed lots of fun tours," Eric said.

"I'll help Danny unload the two horses, and then he can go back to the ranch. I tried to talk Jean into coming with us, but she said riding in a wagon and sleeping in a tent wasn't her idea of a vacation."

Kim set up a small folding table in the shade of a cottonwood tree, retrieved her laptop from the van and started collecting fees. First to arrive was Bruce

Atkins, who'd been a career wrestler before a brace on a wrestling platform had snapped and propelled him several feet into the spectators. His spine was injured, and he'd come to NLC in a wheelchair. Treatments took almost a year, but finally he was able to walk on his own two feet. A hulk of a man weighing over two hundred pounds, his wrestling days were over, but he'd become a successful real estate agent in Denver. His wife, Denise, a tiny, quiet woman, wasn't an outdoor enthusiast, but she went anywhere Bruce wanted to go. Many of the other participants could tell similar stories.

Other staff members arrived before noon. Dr. Alexander and his unmarried sister, Mary, with whom he made his home, had brought Peggy McCane. Connie felt it necessary to have a nurse or doctor with them, and since both members of her medical staff liked the wagon train trip, it worked out well. Fortunately, they'd never needed a doctor, but Peggy had been handy for bruised knees, sore muscles and insect bites.

Charlotte Redmond had once worked at NLC as a trainer, but she'd transferred to a hospital in Kansas, where her parents lived. She'd liked the first wagon trip while she was a member of the staff, and she'd come back this year, bringing her twenty-year-old brother, Leonard.

The youngest member of this year's crew was Bobby Richie, an eighteen-year-old, who'd never had a serious injury but worked out regularly on the weight machines in the gym. After his bicycle tour of the country, Bobby's ambition was to play pro football, and considering his achievements so far, he was well on his way. Observing his six-foot height and muscular body, Connie pitied the horse that had to haul him around for the next five days.

Dorothy Martin was a member of the Marriage First group, and this was her first experience on a wagon train. A career paralegal, Dorothy had no interest in marriage, and the support of the Marriage First group helped her focus on the pitfalls of illicit relations.

Several of the other instructors had registered for the trip, including Russell Bunce, the aerobics instructor at NLC.

By two o'clock everyone had arrived, and Connie directed them to an assembly area in a grove of lodgepole pines, where the wagons were in a circle formation reminiscent of the overland caravans of the past. Everyone was so excited that it was difficult to stop their talking, but Connie blew on the whistle hanging around her neck, and at its shrill tones, conversation ceased.

"Welcome to NLC's fourth annual wagon train excursion. From this point on, we'll be under the guidance of Victor Gregory, the wagon master. As a captain commands his ship, Victor will be in charge here. His orders are to be obeyed even if we don't like them. Listen to his instructions, so we can get underway."

Victor Gregory could easily have stepped out of the nineteenth century. He wore a wide-brimmed hat that had seen better days, faded jeans, a blue cotton shirt, with a red bandanna tied around his neck. Victor had a perpetual slouch, so whether he walked or stood, his posture belied his six-foot plus height.

Faded blue eyes peered out of a brown, lined face. The wagon master wasn't playing a part—he'd ridden the range for fifty years before he retired and turned his holdings into a dude ranch, which was much more profitable and easier than his former occupation had been. But Victor remembered his range-riding days with fondness, and he indulged his memories by organizing a few wagon trips each year.

He leaned against the wheel of one wagon, his blue eyes stern as he surveyed the group before him. "There's only one rule on this wagon train—you do what I say!" Then his eyes twinkled. "But I won't have much to say."

The group applauded, and he tipped his hat.

"However," he drawled, and his audience groaned, "everybody is expected to do a share of the work. I'll give orders necessary to the use of the horses and equipment, and if I find it necessary, I'll change the rules as we go along. My crew will take care of the horses at night. The rest of it is up to you. Miss Connie makes the schedule, assigns duties and gives me my orders." He hunkered down beside the wagon and motioned for Connie to carry on.

"One of the main things for us to remember," she said, "is that we will leave this forest as litter-free as we found it, and in some cases, even cleaner because this area is a favorite place for hikers, who sometimes aren't as conscious of the environment as we intend to be. So, if you see debris thrown away by someone else, I hope you'll pick it up and dispose of it properly.

"I'll post a schedule of activities and workload each morning, but your duties won't be burdensome, for we want you to enjoy the week. Rose, of course, will have cooking duty each day, but her job is supervisory. Some of us will help.''

Getting into the holiday spirit, the group applauded and cheered. "Unless you prefer that I do the cooking," Connie added with a smile.

Her suggestion was greeted with exaggerated boos.

A thirty-year-old woman, one of the more timid patients at NLC, raised her hand hesitantly. "What about wild animals? Will we see any bears?''

Connie motioned to Victor, who slouched to his feet.

"It isn't likely that we'll encounter any dangerous animals, and if you do run into a bear or mountain lion, remember the animals are probably as scared as you are. We'll be camping along the river, and it's possible bears might be nosing around at night. If you see a bear, back off and give the animal room to escape. As for lions, it's rare that they attack people. But to avoid problems, hike in groups and make a lot of noise, so the animals will get out of your way.''

"I have pamphlets, prepared by the Division of Wildlife,'' Kim interjected, "detailing specific instructions about living with wildlife. Each of you should study these pamphlets.''

"We'll rise and shine, at seven o'clock,'' Connie continued. "Breakfast is an hour later. After we clean the campsite, we'll travel for a couple of hours. You can walk, ride in the wagons, or travel on horseback. After a long lunch break, we'll move on for another two to three hours and camp for the night.''

"Connie,'' Russell Bunce said, "I'm planning a half hour of aerobics soon after we circle at the end of the day. I brought tapes along, and I hope all of you will participate. Even if we're saddle weary, the exercise will be beneficial.''

"Thanks, Russell. I didn't expect you to work, but I agree each of us will find it helpful.'' Turning her attention to the others, she said, "If you aren't into aerobics, you can enjoy free time until supper, which is at seven o'clock. The first two days we'll travel along the Cache La Poudre River, where you can fish, and any trout you catch, we'll put on ice to save for a fish fry one night. The last two days, we'll proceed into a wilderness area of scenic beauty. You may want to hike or ride horseback into places our wagons can't go. Wildlife is abundant in this area, especially at dusk and early morning, so have your cameras ready for photo taking. This is designed to be a leisurely trip, so plan to enjoy yourselves. Questions?''

"Any campfires?'' Kim said and grinned.

"Sorry. I forgot campfires. Our day ends by eleven o'clock, but an hour or so before that, we'll have organized activities around a campfire. Russell is handy with a guitar. He plays for us while we sing campfire songs, country-and-western ditties and the like. Tonight, we'll get acquainted—learn about each other, and especially about our connections to NLC.'' She paused. "Kim, you have the list. Please finish for me.''

Kim referred to a paper she took out of a file folder. "Tomorrow night we'll have western stories. They can be truth or fiction, but they must deal with the Old West. Wednesday night is Talent Night, and everyone is expected to do something. The last night, we'll discuss the spiritual lessons we've learned this week. Eric will be in charge of that meeting.''

"Sounds like fun," Bruce Atkins said.

"If I'm not around to answer questions," Connie added, "buttonhole Kim—she has all the answers anyway."

When they got underway, Bruce Atkins drove the first wagon with Denise sitting beside him. His back was still fragile, and his doctors advised him to avoid horseback riding. He volunteered to drive a wagon every day, and for a man who'd spent so much time in the wrestling ring and had never touched a horse until two years ago, he made an efficient teamster.

About half of the group rode horses—others alternately walked or rode in the wagons. The pace was leisurely and the weather pleasant. Driving the second wagon, Connie felt at peace with the world, although an occasional worry about Joseph's legal problems popped into her head. Della, sitting beside Connie, kept a light conversation going, so the drive was peaceful.

Della was a world traveler, and she always had interesting stories about her experiences. Della had a way of finding humor in everything, and when Connie was laughing over the older woman's animated account of her first elephant ride, Della interjected, saying, "I saw Ray Blazer last week."

Connie's laughter stopped immediately, but she didn't comment on Della's statement.

"I met him in a restaurant in Denver, and I had a few choice remarks to make to him about his behavior at NLC, and especially the way he sabotaged your equipment before he left."

"Thank you, Della, but I wish you hadn't said anything to him."

Grinning, she responded, "I didn't speak hastily. I probably considered it two or three seconds before I gave him a piece of my mind. And do you know, honey, I gathered he's sorry he left NLC? He said that his new job isn't working out well, and he intends to leave."

Not sure where this conversation was heading, Connie touched the backs of the horses with her whip, and chose her words carefully. Was Della suggesting she should rehire Ray? "I had no choice but to ask for his resignation," she finally said.

Della nodded. "I realize that, but the point is, do you want him back?"

"No—an unequivocal no! I've forgiven Ray, but he reminds me of things I want to forget, and I couldn't trust him again."

"Well, I just thought I'd ask."

Connie's peace of mind was gone, for at the mention of Ray's name, she remembered how he'd humiliated her, causing her to distrust all men, even Joseph. Should she forget her love for Joseph and go it alone as Dorothy Martin was satisfied to do? Living as a single person had its rewards, she thought. But she didn't think it was right for her.

Joseph wasn't interested in aerobics, and since he didn't have evening duty, as soon as he unhitched from the wagon, he took his fishing gear and headed toward the river. After she'd assigned each person to their tents or wagons and helped them settle in, Connie walked toward the river and sat on the grass to watch Joseph.

He stood knee-deep in the swift stream, and as she watched, he had a strike on his fly, and skillfully brought a brown trout toward him. He dropped the fish in the creel at his waist and cast again.

After a half hour Joseph saw her watching him, and he waved.

"Don't let me bother you," she called. "I came for a walk." She stood up. "I'll see you back at camp."

"No, wait. I'm going to stop soon anyway, and we can walk back together."

After he caught another trout, Joseph waded toward the bank and opened his creel to proudly display his catch.

"Caught four! I'll clean and filet them when we get back to camp."

"If the rest of the fishermen do as well, we'll have a trout fry one night."

"A few months ago, I thought my trout fishing days were over. I owe you a lot, Connie."

Was gratitude the only emotion he felt for her?

"You did the work—direction and encouragement were my only contributions. Any other trainer could have done the same."

He shook his head. "No, healing required confidence in the trainer, and I might not have been so confident of another trainer. I'm so thankful to have a whole body again, I could shout my praises from the tops of the mountains."

"Why don't you?" she asked with a smile.

"I've said a lot of silent praise to God, in case you wondered," he answered, giving her hand a squeeze.

The trip proceeded as planned, without any hitches, and after they reached a wilderness area on Thursday, Russell Bunce organized a hike along a moderately difficult trail, usually frequented by four-wheel-drive vehicles. Besides Russell, seven other members of the caravan elected to take the hike, including Connie, Joseph, Dr. Alexander, Peggy, the Redmonds and Bobby Richie. The wagons would continue their daily travel, and the hikers planned to meet the caravan at another point farther along the trail.

Russell had scouted out this trail the year before, and he instructed the hikers as they gathered at six o'clock in the morning. "This isn't an easy trail, and since we won't all hike at the same speed, we won't try to stay in one group, but two people should always be together in case of an emergency. I've prepared maps for you, so it shouldn't be difficult to find your way. We'll regroup when we reach the mesa, which is a good place to rest, for it's a lovely spot with a view. The trail crosses several streams, and if it should rain, be alert for rapidly rising water."

Joseph moved to Connie's side. "Want to be my partner?"

"Sure. We've done a lot of hiking together."

"Yeah, when I was dragging along behind. I intend to keep up with you today."

"You set the pace. I'll follow."

"Rose got up early to have some breakfast ready for you," Russell announced. "You'll find coffee, biscuits and a Mexican omelette at the chuck wagon. Be ready to go in a half hour.''

The hikers started out before the other campers got up, but Joseph couldn't resist scratching on the side of the tent where Kim and Eric slept. Kim stuck her tousled head out of the opening.

''Just because you want to punish yourselves is no reason to disturb us,'' she said. ''You guys are supposed to be on vacation, and you're taking a busman's holiday.''

''To each his own,'' Connie called. ''Keep the wagons rolling.''

Joseph had exchanged his cowboy boots for rugged hiking shoes, and he wore a short-sleeved T-shirt and jeans, and a baseball cap. A long-sleeved sweatshirt hung from his backpack. Connie opted for denim shorts, a cotton blouse, woolen socks and walking boots. She wondered momentarily if she should have brought heavier clothing, but the last two days had been hot, and she didn't anticipate any need for warmer clothes. Connie watched Joseph's gait, and although he occasionally favored his left leg, he walked easily and without effort. They carried walking sticks to help them over rough places in the trail, or to ward off a wild animal if necessary.

Several of the inclines were rugged and steep, and they stopped often for breathing spells. Occasionally they saw some of the other couples ahead of them, and the Redmonds trailing behind, stopping often to take pictures of the flowers along the trail.

By noon, they reached the mesa that afforded a panoramic view of Poudre Canyon and parts of Rocky Mountain National Park, where the other hikers rested. Russell Bunce approached them. "Since we've made such good time, some of us plan to climb higher and take another road back to the wagons." After outlining the alternate route on the map, Russell added, "It's a little risky, Joseph, for some streams in this area flood easily, so be careful if we have a downpour."

After Russell rejoined his companions, Joseph asked, "Do you want to take the extra miles?"

"Right now, I'm too tired to consider any extra walking. Let's rest awhile," Connie said with a laugh, "and then make the decision."

Putting their packs aside, they stretched out on the grass. When they awakened, they were alone on the mesa. "I didn't expect to sleep so long," Connie said. "I guess the others have gone on."

"Except the Redmonds—I see them downhill quite a ways."

While they ate their lunch in companionable silence, Connie thought that in spite of the time they'd spent together in the last four months, she knew very little about Joseph. What did he do as a child? What were his aspirations for the future?

"Have you always lived in this area?" she asked.

"Yes. My great-grandfather homesteaded the ranch where Jean lives. My father added property to the family's holdings, as did his father, so when my parents retired, Jean and I split the property and bought it from our parents. Our semiannual payments provide funds for them to live in a retirement home near San Francisco. Jean lives in the ranch house that my grandfather built. The house on my section wasn't much, but I lived in it while I was at the university, and built the new house before I got married.''

''Is Jean a widow?''

''No. She's divorced. My parents are disappointed in both of us.'' He grinned. ''They want some grand-children—my mother says she's intimidated by all the grandmothers in their community who have pictures to show.'' He paused, adding, ''Virginia didn't want children, and under the circumstances, it's just as well.''

He stared into the distance, and Connie wished she hadn't probed into his past. It had disturbed Joseph, and she'd learned things she wished she hadn't. The dismal tone in his voice when he talked about Virginia could be indicative of two things—he still loved her, or she had disappointed him greatly. Perhaps both. Hoping to dispel his somber mood, she contin-ued. ''What about your childhood? You mentioned that your parents made you learn a lot of Scripture verses.''

He smiled. ''Yes, and I resented having to spend Sunday afternoon in the house when my friends were fishing or biking. My father was strict about Sunday. We didn't work, nor shop, nor do much of anything. We worshiped, meditated and rested. More than once, when our parents took their habitual Sunday after-noon naps, Jean and I slipped down to the creek and went swimming. I always suspected our mother knew it, but if Dad had caught us, we'd have known.'' He chuckled. ''Dad had never heard of child abuse, and he swatted the seat of my pants more than once.'' He took a drink of water, recapped the bottle and placed it in his backpack.

"We had a good childhood, although I didn't think so at the time, for when I was in my teens, Dad put me to work on the ranch. I was in 4-H and played softball for our high school, so it wasn't all work. We didn't travel though, and I've always been sorry about that. I go to see my parents in California once a year, but that's the extent of my traveling."

"Ranching is a year-round job, I'm sure."

"Yes, it is, but it's the life for me." Joseph pulled his cap lower on his forehead. "Have you always lived in Colorado, Connie?"

"After I was five years old. We'd lived in Wyoming before that, but Dad was transferred to Denver, and we've lived here ever since."

"What did you do as a child?"

"I didn't have an active childhood because of my physical problem, and my medical bills were expensive, so we didn't travel, either. I have one sister, who's married, and lives on the East Coast. She comes with her husband and two boys to visit us every year, so we haven't gone there. It sounds as if you and I may have been deprived of some things in our childhood, but we're both fortunate to have had caring parents, who gave us security."

Joseph reached for her hand and squeezed it. "And we still have them—I'm thankful for that." He scrambled to his feet, and held her hand and drew her upward.

"Are we going to take the long way back to the wagons?"

With a sigh, Connie said, "I'm willing. Actually, I'd like to stay here the rest of the day and do nothing. Right now, I'm duty free, but my work starts again when we get back to the wagons. We should move on, though, for the longer route may take more time than we expect."

Charlotte and Leonard Redmond reached the mesa, and Connie said, "Here's a map Russell left for you. The rest of us are going to take this longer route back to the wagons." She pointed it out to the siblings. "If you travel the short route, follow the red arrows on the map."

"We'll eat our lunch, rest and then decide," Charlotte said. "We stopped to take so many pictures that we're later than the rest of you. We'll probably return the shortest way."

"Okay," Connie said. "If you do take the long route, that trail is marked with round green dots. See you back at the wagons."

"Forward march," Joseph said, a smile breaking across his face. Connie loved it when he forgot his troubles and let his natural, friendly personality surface.

"Lead the way," she said. "It's probably a long way back to the wagons."

Chapter Ten

The first storm came two hours after Joseph and Connie left the mesa. The sudden downpour started without warning, and both of them were wet before they could retrieve ponchos from their packs and pull them over their heads. It rained for fifteen minutes, but they kept plodding downward, avoiding slick spots on the path as much as possible.

When the sun came out, they were on the bank of a small stream.

"Let's take off these ponchos and hope our clothes dry in the sun," Joseph said. "We should cross this creek before it rises any more."

"Russell mentioned some challenging streams. I wonder how many more there are? I'm a little worried—probably we should have taken the shorter route. These showers may continue."

Joseph took off his cap, and slapped it against his thigh to get rid of the water. Looking at the sky, he said, "You may be right, but we've come too far this way to retrace our steps—let's hope for the best."

Joseph went upstream a short distance looking for a shallow ford, but when muddy water started roiling from the mountain, he rejoined Connie. "We'll have to cross here right away." He rolled up his pant legs and sat down to take off his shoes. Connie removed her boots, tied the strings together and slung them around her neck.

"It's no more than a foot deep here."

Joseph agreed. "But it's swift and deeper than our shoe tops, and I don't want cold, wet feet as well as wet clothing. Ready?"

"I left my socks on because I have an extra pair in my pack. Those rocks look slick, and the socks will give me some leverage. Let's go."

Connie gasped when she stepped into the icy water, and Joseph, leading the way, shouted, "Wow! Talk about cold feet!"

The stream, only fifteen feet wide, seemed easy to ford, and they'd almost reached the other bank when Joseph fell to his knees and was submerged to his waist. Connie grabbed his arm, he struggled to his feet and they reached the bank without further mishap.

Concerned, Connie asked quickly, "Did you hurt your hip?"

With water dripping from his rolled-up jeans, Joseph ran his hands over his left hip and thigh. "I don't feel any pain, but my knees sting."

He had a cut on his left knee, and Connie took a first-aid kit from her backpack and cleansed the wound with an antibacterial wipe. Joseph winced when she applied a disinfectant and ointment to the bruised area.

"You're persecuting me again, Doc."

"Pardon me!" Connie replied in mock anger. "The next time, I'll let your leg bleed."

Connie sat on a rock, replaced her wet socks with dry ones and put on her shoes. Joseph rolled down the legs of his jeans. "I wish I'd brought an extra pair of pants. My shirt may dry, but these jeans won't. We're going to have a miserable hike the rest of the way."

Hearing thunder in the distance, Connie said, "And if we have more rain, we may find other flooded streams." She looked at the crude map Russell had given them. "It looks as if there may be three more creeks. I wonder how the others are getting along. Russell does a lot of backpacking, so he won't be taken by surprise, but I don't think the Redmonds have had much wilderness experience."

"They didn't seem interested in coming this way, and the other trail isn't so risky."

The rain held off until they reached the first stream, which was strewn with large boulders. They crossed it easily by jumping from one rock to another. When the rain became a steady downpour, Connie started worrying. They were a long way from the wagons, and their progress was slow because the roadbed was slippery. What if they had to spend the night in the mountains? She couldn't be alone with Joseph all night. Perhaps some of the other hikers couldn't make it across the streams either, and several of them could camp together.

With water lapping at their heels, they crossed the

second of the three streams, teetering and tottering on a large log that had been placed from bank to bank. Joseph shouted above the roar of the water, "Russell probably put that across."

"Only one more creek to go," she said.

They'd just reached the other side when a large wave washed over the log and dislodged it, hurtling it downstream. There wouldn't be any way to return over this route. They traveled for another hour, but halted beside the last stream. Judging from the map, Connie knew they couldn't be more than three miles from where the wagons were parked for the night. She looked around anxiously, hoping to see some of their other companions, but the area was vacant except for her and Joseph.

"This creek is still rising," Joseph said, "so it will be several hours before it's fordable, and it'll be dark before that. We'll have to stay here tonight."

"There has to be another place to ford the stream," Connie said desperately.

Joseph motioned to the steep mountain terrain. "The only possible crossing is high on that mountain, and I'm too tired to look for it. I've had all the walking I can take today."

"The others will worry about us."

"I doubt it. Russell will know the situation. It's going to be a cold and wet night, but I think we're stuck here."

She couldn't be here all night with Joseph. What would people think?

"I wish I knew something about this area. There might be a shelter close by," Joseph continued. "We'll be miserable before morning. Neither of us are dressed warmly, and I assume you don't have a blanket in your backpack,'' he added jokingly, but Connie didn't find the situation amusing.

She didn't answer, desperately looking back along the trail, hoping that the Redmonds had followed them and would be along soon. But after several minutes of indecision, she conceded that she'd been plunged into an awkward position through no fault of her own, and she would have to deal with it.

"I see a small rock outcropping up the mountain a short distance that might provide a little shelter,'' Joseph said.

She nodded agreement, and he slowly led the way up the steep incline. The ledge jutted a few feet from the rock formation above it, and although the ground was damp, at least the rain wouldn't pour directly on them, and they would be safe from lightning. Connie removed her poncho and backpack. Her clothes hadn't had a chance to dry, and she was cold, hungry, miserable and tense.

"I don't have much food left, but I still have a full bottle of water,'' she said, trying to speak calmly.

"I'm carrying matches in my pack, but there isn't any dry wood, so I guess we can't have a fire. I'm sorry I can't provide a better solution, Connie.''

"It isn't your fault.'' Without looking at him, she started laying out the food in her pack. "I have an apple, half of a cheese sandwich and a package of raisins.''

"I was greedier than you at lunchtime. I ate my whole sandwich, but I have a package of cookies and a banana. There's also a container of orange juice. Not enough for a banquet, but we won't starve.''

They ate before it got completely dark, but the easy camaraderie they'd shared throughout the day was missing. Joseph made several attempts at conversation, but when Connie responded in monosyllables, he lapsed into silence also. When all the food was gone, Connie put all the wrappers and containers in her pack and leaned against the rock wall, staring out into the gathering dusk.

"Connie, the only way for us to have any comfort at all tonight is to split our ponchos—put one on the ground, lie on it and use the other for a cover. That won't be very comfortable, but by lying together, our body heat will keep us warm."

She wouldn't meet his eyes. "No. I won't do it. I'll put on my poncho and sit up all night. You can do what you want to do."

"I don't understand you, Connie. I'm not suggesting anything immoral. I told you I'm not that kind of person. Don't you trust me?"

"The Bible says to refrain from all appearance of evil. If anyone ever heard we slept together, they'd think the worst."

"Who's going to know? There's no one here but us, and I won't comment on what we do."

She shook her head.

"Connie, you're judging me by the actions of Ray. Just because he tried to force his attentions on you after you broke your engagement is no reason to think I'm the same kind of person."

She turned surprised, angry eyes on him. "How did you know about that?"

"Eric told me. He heard Ray bragging to another staff member about the way he'd grabbed you and had given you some passionate kisses, so you wouldn't forget him. When you ran away from me that day, I talked to Eric—trying to make some sense of the way you'd acted. He advised me to give you time to forget Ray's indiscretion. I've tried to be a friend to you, and except for one misguided statement I shouldn't have made, I don't think my behavior has been out of line.''

Connie reached for her poncho, tied it around her body and scooted as far away from Joseph as she could while remaining under the rock shelter. Lying down with her backpack for a pillow, she said bitterly, ''As you've pointed out, I'm the one with the problem. I have to do what I think is right. Good night, Joseph.'' She turned her back on him. The ground was hard and cold, and she couldn't help thinking of the comfort she could find in Joseph's arms.

She'd carefully guarded the facts about that morning, soon after she'd broken her engagement, when she'd encountered Ray on her early morning run. She was strong, but no match for the muscular Ray, who'd grabbed her and kissed her repeatedly in an insulting manner. When he'd seen Peggy McCane jogging down the path, Ray had left her with a taunting laugh.

His attitude had left her skeptical of men in general, and she'd made up her mind to steer clear of any future involvements and concentrate on her worthwhile career. Her vocation was a calling from God, and that was what He wanted her to do. She could devote full priority to it if she didn't marry. Joseph's arrival at NLC had changed all of that, and not for the first time, she wished she hadn't learned to love him.

With her back to Joseph, she didn't know what preparations he made for the night. Her uneasy mind, as well as the discomfort of her body, kept Connie awake, and she squirmed on the hard ground. The area was littered with stone fragments, and every way she moved, a rock gouged her body somewhere. The rain stopped, and the sky glistened with stars. Her depression lightened to think that the streams would be fordable in the morning.

Obsessed with the need to know what time it was, as quietly as she could, Connie unzipped her pack and took out a small flashlight, hoping the batteries weren't dead. Covering the flash with her poncho, she turned on the light to look at her watch.

Twelve o'clock!

She hadn't slept at all, but she'd had plenty of time to think. Connie sat up and eased her back against the rock wall. When her eyes adjusted to the darkness, she made out Joseph lying on his side, facing the other way. As she watched, he flexed his left leg, and she knew he was uncomfortable.

"Are you awake, Joseph?" she whispered, not wanting to awaken him if he slept.

"Yes. I can't get comfortable enough to sleep."

"Neither can I. I checked my watch, and it's only midnight, so it's a long time until daylight."

"Yes."

"The rain has stopped though, so we should be able to cross the creeks in the morning."

"That's what I think." He turned, and leaned on his elbow, looking toward her. His voice was reserved, as if he didn't care whether or not he talked to her.

"I hadn't told anyone, not even Kim, about Ray's insulting behavior," Connie said. "And you're right, I had no reason to suspect you of behaving the same way. I apologize, not only for the way I acted tonight, but also for ever believing I couldn't trust you. I've botched everything, including the way I reacted to tonight's situation. I hope you'll forgive me."

"Connie, there's nothing to forgive. I'm not angry with you. I've been worrying over what *I* had done to make you mistrust me."

So far, she'd muffed every opportunity to have a close relationship with Joseph. What if she never had another chance? She moved gingerly across the uneven ground toward him, and he sat up, his open arms waiting. She leaned against him, and his arms pulled her close.

"I do trust you," she said, "with my life, my reputation, my virtue."

He eased her head gently to his shoulder, and secure and comfortable, both of them slept at last.

Connie awakened alone, muscles aching from her cramped sitting position. She saw Joseph down by the creek, but from this angle, she couldn't tell if the water had fallen enough for them to cross. The ledge was too low for her to stand, so she crawled away from it before she stood, groaning with the effort. Any other time she'd slept on the ground, she'd been tucked in a soft bedroll. The last few hours, relaxing in Joseph's arms, had taken away some discomfort, but she still had aches all over her body.

Joseph saw her and called, "Probably another hour

before we can cross. I'll come up for my pack, and we can be ready."

When he reached the ledge, he leaned over and kissed her. "I thought you'd have breakfast ready by now."

She made a face at him. "Don't even mention food. I'll bet Rose is preparing biscuits, hash browns and gravy this morning, and we're going to miss it. We should have saved some of the food we ate last night."

They took their belongings to the creek bank, and sat down to wait, luxuriating in the warm sun that shone around them. A half hour later, Joseph said, "I hear horses," and in a few minutes, riders came into view around a curve in the trail.

"That's Victor Gregory!" Connie shouted.

"And two of his men," Joseph added. "They're leading our mounts. They've come to get us."

Connie, her aches forgotten, stood up and waved. "Am I glad we don't have to walk back to the wagons!"

Victor halted his horses and shouted, "Don't you know how to swim?"

"Don't try to be funny," Connie said. "We've spent a miserable night. Did all the others get back okay?"

"We had to ferry the Redmonds across a creek, and by that time, it was dark. Kim wanted me to come and find you, but as dark as it was, and with more rain threatening, we might have missed you. I figured Mr. Caldwell knew enough about this country that you'd survive all right."

Victor took the reins of the extra horses and

splashed across the stream. "Kim sent you dry clothes, Connie, and Eric took some jeans and a shirt out of your pack, Caldwell. They're in my saddlebags, along with a thermos of coffee and some sandwiches that Rose sent."

They sipped on the hot coffee and devoured the sandwiches before Connie went downstream, Joseph upstream to change their clothes behind some bushes. Last night Connie couldn't see anything positive about their delay. Now she would always be thankful for this forced sojourn as the time she'd learned to trust Joseph.

Connie's apprehensions—that their companions would question her and Joseph about what had happened during the hours they spent alone on the mountain—were soon alleviated. When they returned to the spot where the wagons were parked, everyone was in an uproar.

Bobby Richie raced toward them when the riders came into sight. When they stopped their horses, he said to Victor, "A bear came into camp this morning."

Victor laughed at him. "I'm surprised you'd be upset about a little thing like that. It's not unusual to see bears here in the forest."

But his laughter turned to concern when Bobby added, "When Bruce discharged a pistol into the air to scare the beast away, it bolted into the horse corral and spooked the horses. They broke through the rope fence and scattered."

Victor wheeled his mount and glanced around the meadow. Horses dotted the wide landscape.

"Great!" Victor said in disgust. "Not all of them are in sight, so we'll have to comb the woods until we find them." He shouted orders to his men to saddle up and prepare to round up the animals.

"No moving until we find all of them, Connie," the wagon master snapped. "Too bad this had to happen on our last day."

"Is there anything we can do to help?" she asked.

"No, I don't want a bunch of greenhorns in the way. My men can handle it." He turned to Joseph. "We can use you, Caldwell, if you're up to it."

Connie didn't think Joseph should be working after the tiresome night they'd spent, but he would be experienced in rounding up horses. With Eric's help, Rose quickly prepared sandwiches for Victor's workers.

After the riders left camp, Connie told Kim, "Tell everyone that we'll stay here until Victor gives the word. They can go on short hikes, but stay close. We'll fire three shots as a signal that everyone should come back to camp."

"Connie, come to the campfire," Rose called, "I saved some breakfast for you."

"As soon as I wash up. I've had enough of being muddy."

"Couldn't you find shelter for the night?" Eric said, and that was the only question she heard.

"We sat under a small rock ledge that protected us from the rain, but we were already wet before we learned we couldn't cross the last creek."

By noon, the horses were rounded up, and Victor gave orders to move forward. He knew a shorter trail to the camping area where they always spent the last night of their trek, and they arrived in plenty of time to prepare their meal.

After supper, the trekkers gathered around a campfire that Leonard Redmond and Bobby Richie had built. Being the youngest of the group, the two boys had formed a close bond of friendship. To make their last evening together a comfortable one, Victor's workers had brought wooden benches to the area the day before, and these were placed in a circle around the fire. By now, the group looked ragged. Most of the men hadn't shaved since they left home, and the clothing that had been neatly pressed when they'd set out Monday morning was stained with grime and perspiration. It wasn't easy to keep clean on the wagon trip, and Connie thought how difficult it must have been for pioneers who were on the trail for months.

The program started out on a light note with the campers telling of amusing incidents of the week. Bruce Atkins said, "Dorothy Martin sprinted for her tent as fast as a deer when that bear moseyed into camp."

Dorothy's face flushed, but she didn't deny it.

Numerous campfire songs resounded throughout the small cove, reminding Connie of her childhood and the church camps she'd attended. After several interesting testimonials from the group about incidents of the week that had inspired them to undertake a closer walk with God, Eric took charge of the service.

By this time, darkness had set in, with the camp

lighted only by the dying embers of the fire. A sliver
of moon peered over the hill, and a few stars sparkled
in the darkening sky. A soft breeze caressed them,
stirring up puffs of smoke from the fire.

Into this peaceful setting, Eric's deep voice gave
new meaning to the Eighth Psalm. "When I consider
Your heavens, the work of Your fingers, the moon
and the stars, which You have set in place, what is
man that You are mindful of him, the son of man that
You care for him? You made him a little lower than
the heavenly beings and crowned him with glory and
honor."

He paused to let the beauty of the words penetrate
their minds and hearts. In the distance, Connie heard
the horses stamping and snorting, and, all around
them, in subdued tones, insects chirped incessantly.
But the people sat in silence, while peace and qui-
etude hovered over them. It was a reverent moment.

"This is my first camping trip," Eric said. "I've
always been amazed that our omnipotent God, the
Everlasting Father, concerns Himself with finite hu-
mans such as we are. Yet, the Psalmist says that He
does. And never have I been more appreciative of the
greatness of God than I've been this week when I've
seen the wonders of the Creator all around me. The
mountains, the rivers, the thunderstorms all speak of
God. How could any of us not have been touched by
the wonder of the Creator? How can any of us go
back to our everyday lives without making Him Lord
of our life?"

As Eric continued to extol the greatness of God,
Connie rededicated anew her life to His service. She

fully believed that God had called her to a ministry of physical and spiritual therapy, and she longed to be even more fully committed to that service. But how would Joseph fit in with her calling? He had his own work at the ranch, and as far as she could see, their two vocations didn't complement each other. And doubts still crept into her mind about marriage. If she married, Joseph was the one, but could she be more dedicated to her calling if she remained single?

"To close our vespers tonight," Eric said, "I've asked Joseph to sing, 'How Great Thou Art.' He reluctantly agreed, saying he isn't a soloist, but I've heard him sing in chapel services, and I believe he can do it."

His face covered with brown stubble, and clothed in his wrinkled jeans and shirt, Joseph only faintly resembled the neatly tailored man she'd known for several months. As he sang in a rich baritone about the stars, the rolling thunder, the forest glades, sweetly singing birds, lofty mountain grandeur and gentle breezes, Connie listened, hand on her pulsing throat. He typified all she could want in a friend or husband. Despite the hurdles that they had to overcome, she believed that if it was God's will for them to be together, He would provide the way.

No one moved for several minutes after Joseph finished singing, and then Eric closed the service by saying, "And all God's people said…" and the campground resounded with their voices when the whole group shouted in unison, "Amen!"

Danny Keller waited with Joseph's stock trailer when they arrived at the campground, and while he loaded his two horses and gear, Connie said goodbye to each member of the group. It was a bittersweet moment for her—she was eager to continue her work at NLC and looking forward to helping Joseph solve the mystery of Virginia's death, but after a week away from the intrusion of the world, it was hard to go back to everyday problems. By the time she waved the last vehicle on its way, Victor had his horses loaded in trailers and his wagons secured on flatbed trucks. While Kim settled accounts with Victor, Connie walked to Joseph's truck, where he and Eric talked, but Eric soon strolled away. Joseph took her hand.

"Thanks for asking me to go on this tour, Connie. I'm going home spiritually and mentally refreshed, with new hope for the future. As far as I can see, all that stands in the way of our happiness is the question of Virginia's death. Settling that is my main priority. Are you sure you still want to be mixed up in that? It might become dangerous if we get close to the real killer—if there is one."

"What troubles you troubles me. I'm committed to clearing you of this suspicion, and although I don't know how, I believe your innocence will be proven. Trust God for the results. A good Bible verse to consider in your situation is from the book of Proverbs. 'In all your ways acknowledge Him, *and* He will make your paths straight.'"

Glancing around to see if anyone watched, Joseph leaned forward and planted a quick kiss on her lips. "I'll telephone you soon. I intend to make an appointment with George, if he'll see me, and I think he will if I tell him I want to give Virginia's jewelry to his daughter. In the meantime, I'll try to get a lead on Debbie Smith. She may hold the key to this whole mystery.''

Chapter Eleven

Joseph telephoned Thursday evening. "I've just talked to George," he reported, "and he reluctantly agreed to see me Saturday afternoon. While we're there, I intend to confront him with the newspaper clipping Rose found. I've also learned that Debbie Smith is back in Colorado, and we might be able to see her Sunday. She has an unlisted telephone, so we'll just drop in on her. Be sure and bring that photo with you when we see her. I'll pick you up at noon, if that's convenient."

Connie had almost two days to think about that upcoming interview. Since Kim's marriage, she and Eric had moved into a cozy apartment in Lakewood, and Connie spent many lonely evenings. She and Kim had been inseparable for years, and although they were together most of the day, she missed the chats they'd enjoyed every evening before they went to sleep.

Connie thought that Joseph loved her, even though

he hadn't said so, and she started dreaming of the day when they might marry and live together. But where? If Joseph lived on the ranch and she was at NLC, they couldn't enjoy the closeness that Kim and Eric knew—being together at work and at night, too.

Without Kim to talk to when she was alone in the apartment, Connie spent more time reading the Bible and praying for guidance. Until Connie had fallen in love with Joseph, she'd seldom fretted about anything, but where he was concerned, she didn't have much self-control. She feared he wouldn't recover from his disability, she worried that he still loved his wife, she fretted because he couldn't find out what had killed Virginia—and she was tormented with the possibility that Joseph might have to go to prison.

Frustrations like these were not representative of a mature Christian faith, and she worried about that, too. After searching the Scriptures for hours to find some answer to her situation, Connie finally came upon a message the Apostle Paul had sent to the Philippians. "Do not be anxious about anything, but in everything, by prayer and petition, with thanksgiving, present your requests to God. And the peace of God, which transcends all understanding, will guard your hearts and your minds in Christ Jesus."

"Father," she prayed, relief flooding her heart, "forgive me. I seem to forget that *You're* in control. God, I submit to You. I can't stop wondering what the future holds for Joseph and me, but I promise I won't spend any more sleepless nights worrying about it. Thanks for Your Word, and the assurance it brings to the weary and restless heart. Amen."

Believing that whatever happened, she and Joseph

could accept it, Connie looked forward to learning the cause of Virginia's death as soon as possible. When Joseph came for her on Saturday, she was singing as he entered her office, and he commented, "It's been weeks since I've heard you sing. I've missed it."

"I can't sing when I'm worrying, and that's what I've been doing for weeks, but no more." She shared with him the Scripture she'd read the night before.

"Then we'll sing a duet while we're driving to George's house—I need something to bolster my courage."

"Do you know the hymn, 'Great Is Thy Faithfulness'?" Connie asked.

"Yes. My father used to sing that as a solo in our worship services."

"I've been singing one verse of that song over and over this morning—the one stressing that God will provide all our needs. The message of the whole song speaks to the yearnings of my heart—we can sing that together as we travel."

Joseph agreed, and while they drove along the busy streets, they didn't dread the coming ordeal, for they sang of the abiding presence of God, who provided blessings in the midst of adversity.

The Perrys' three-story Spanish-style house built of pink stucco dominated the small lot on which it stood in an exclusive suburb of Denver.

"Virginia's father had this house built about fifty years ago," Joseph said as he stopped his truck in the driveway. "Seems strange to be coming here again. A lot has happened since Christmas when Virginia and I came for dinner, only a few weeks before she was killed.''

''And all seemed well then?''

''As I look back on it, I'm not so sure. There seemed to be unusual tension between George and Virginia, but it was the first Christmas we'd spent together since their father had died, and I thought they were sorrowing because he was gone.''

Picking up a jewelry chest from the back seat, Joseph sighed deeply. ''We might as well go in. I dread it. Thanks for coming with me—I can use your support.'' Connie lifted his hand and kissed it.

''You know I'm on your side,'' she assured him with a smile.

A maid in a dark-brown dress answered the door and ushered Joseph and Connie through a wide central hall. They bypassed a curved, free-hanging stairway, and entered a brightly furnished, cozy sitting room that overlooked a broad sweeping flower garden. A tall man, who had features similar to the pictures she'd seen of Virginia, laid aside a paper he'd been reading and stood.

''Good afternoon, Joseph,'' he said stiffly, but made no move toward them, nor did he invite them to be seated. A rather plump, plain woman entered the room from a small dinette, but she gave them no greeting.

''George, this is my friend, Connie Harmon. Connie, meet George and Stephanie Perry.''

''Hello,'' Connie said. Stephanie didn't speak. George nodded.

''Sit down, Connie,'' Joseph said, and stepping forward, he took a chair close to the one George had occupied on their entrance. "It just now occurred to me that I have as much right to be here as anyone else. Virginia owned half of this house, and as her heir, that portion belongs to me."

Connie sat on a small sofa, uneasy at Joseph's words, fearful of how the Perrys would react. He shouldn't antagonize them. George shifted his feet, muttered an oath and dropped into his chair. Stephanie perched on the edge of the sofa where Connie sat, and murmured, "Hello."

"So that's why you came here," George said angrily. "Mentioned the jewelry, so you could get your foot in the door. You know I'd not have let you in otherwise."

"It's true, I did use the jewelry as a lure, but I hadn't even thought about the ownership of this house until this moment. I've had too much else to concern me to worry about ownership of the Perry home. But I have the jewels." He handed the chest to his brother-in-law. "Virginia inherited most of your mother's jewelry, and I thought your daughter should have them. I don't know if Virginia disposed of any of the items. I kept a turquoise necklace, and a few pieces I'd bought, for they're hardly in the price range of Virginia's other jewelry, and wouldn't mean anything to your daughter."

George riffled through the box, and he held up a long silver chain bearing a single diamond pendant. "This belonged to my grandmother. My mother wore it on her wedding day, as did Virginia. I would like for Heather to wear it at her wedding. I thank you for bringing them back."

George handed the chest to Stephanie. "Would you know if he's taken anything?"

"No, George. I have no idea how much jewelry your sister had."

Connie saw a nervous tick in Joseph's forehead, and she knew it was difficult for him to control his temper.

"I didn't take any of her jewelry except the few items I mentioned. George, I can't understand why you've turned on me like this. I thought we would be friends for life. How can you suspect me of taking Virginia's life?"

"That note sounded like it. If you didn't kill her, who did?"

"That's assuming, of course, that she wasn't killed in the accident. But you're asking the question that someone should have asked long ago. I had absolutely nothing to do with Virginia's death, nor did I take one dollar of her inheritance. The authorities have wasted several months suspecting me, and this delay has allowed the real culprit to cover his trail. Now that I've recovered from my injury," he looked at Connie, "thanks to Miss Harmon and her staff at NLC, I intend to do some detective work. I intend to get to the bottom of this situation and prove my innocence." He took the news clipping from his pocket. "Do you know anything about this?"

George took the piece of paper, barely looked at it, and handed it back to Joseph, hardly meeting his eyes. "No."

Connie thought he was lying.

"I think you do," Joseph said, returning the paper to his pocket. "Let's see if I can get a more satisfactory answer to my next question. Why didn't you or your parents tell me about the year Virginia spent away from home, and about the weeks she was sick and under the care of a special nurse, after she returned?''

George squirmed in his chair. ''It wasn't my place to tell you. That was up to Virginia.''

''I'm sure it wouldn't have changed my mind about marrying Virginia, for I loved her, but you should have warned me about her unstable character.''

Connie closed her eyes, and momentarily lost the gist of the conversation, for Joseph's words seared her heart like a hot iron. She'd never heard him say before that he loved Virginia. *God,* she prayed silently, *take away this jealousy of a dead woman. I wouldn't want a husband who'd married someone he didn't love, so I should be grateful that he loved his first wife. If we do marry, I can't have Virginia's memory standing between us all the time.*

She opened her eyes, as Joseph continued, ''If I'd known about her weaknesses, I'd have watched her more closely. What was wrong with Virginia when she came back home?''

George shook his head. ''I don't know.''

''It's pretty obvious that you and your father set me up for the wedding—you knew Virginia had problems and you handed them over to me.''

''She was crazy about you,'' Stephanie said, speaking at last. ''Everyone thought she'd straighten up when you were married.''

George threw an angry glance in her direction, and Stephanie said no more.

A dainty little girl came into the room and stared

at them through vivid green eyes. She scrambled up on her mother's lap, and Connie saw a resemblance to Virginia's pictures.

"Heather," Stephanie said, "you remember your uncle Joseph, don't you?"

"Hello, Heather," Joseph said, and the child stuck out her tongue and ran from the room.

Joseph laughed. "Nobody in the family seems to welcome me." He took the clipping out of his pocket again. "But back to this picture. The informant who gave it to me thinks that one of these people is Virginia, and I'm almost convinced that it is her picture. If so, she was involved in a robbery during the year she bummed around the country. I also think that someone who knew about that holdup blackmailed her after your father died. The bank records show that she withdrew large sums of money, starting shortly after your father's death. George, are you going to help me prove that, or do you want to spend the rest of your life suspecting me and let the real criminal go free?"

"I don't know anything about that paper, I tell you," George said angrily. "I don't know where her money went. I didn't get any of it, either." He stood again. "So, if you've said all you came to say, I'll ask you to leave."

Joseph stood, and reached out his hand to Connie.

"And I don't appreciate you bringing another woman in here so soon after my sister's death." George said angrily. "You could have mourned Virginia for a decent time."

"Connie isn't 'another woman.' She's my physical

therapist, friend and fellow detective," Joseph said. "She's helping me solve this crime."

Showing more spunk than Connie thought she had, Stephanie walked with them to the door, and she shook hands with both Connie and Joseph. "This is my home, too," she said, "and you're welcome to come here whenever you want. I apologize for George—he hasn't been the same since Virginia's death. He was very fond of his sister."

"Yes, I know that," Joseph said.

"Thanks also for bringing the jewelry for Heather. My father made his money himself. His ancestors were poor, so we have no family heirlooms. I'll keep these safe for my daughter."

Connie waved to Stephanie as they backed out of the driveway. "She certainly surprised me. I thought, at first, that she was under George's thumb."

Joseph laughed lightly, and drawled, "George thought she was, too, but he learned after he married her that Stephanie isn't a doormat. She can be pushed only so far before she balks."

They drove a few blocks, and Joseph pulled into a park and stopped under a shade tree.

"What are your impressions of the visit?" he asked.

"George lied about the picture, and I think he knows more than he's telling. He's also afraid for you to investigate this further."

"I expected the latter, because if the news about a blackmailer leaks out, it will smear the reputation of a family that has been prominent in Colorado since the territorial period. I hope I can learn the truth and divert suspicion from myself without hurting George, but when he won't be honest with me, I have to protect myself. He knows very well what Virginia did while she was away from home, but he won't tell me."

"You thought there was some tension between George and Virginia last Christmas. Could they have had trouble over the estate?"

"It's possible that when Virginia's money was all gone, she wanted him to divide the funds they held jointly, and they quarreled over that. And it surprised me that Virginia's portrait has been removed from that room. Her parents had her portrait painted when she was sixteen, and it's hung over the mantel as long as I've been in the family. I'd like to know why it's been taken down, but the whole room has been redecorated, so perhaps I'm imagining things."

"I thought that was a Monet hanging over the mantel, so they must have spent a lot of money redoing the room. Perhaps Stephanie wants the house to reflect her personality rather than the Perrys. Or it might be that, after Virginia was killed, George found it too painful to see her face every day."

Connie believed God had heard and answered her prayer, for it seemed easier to speak dispassionately of Virginia.

"I guess our next move is to find Debbie Smith. Are you free to go with me tomorrow?" Joseph asked.

"Yes, but not until after church. I'm going to worship with my parents in the morning. Would you like to come with us?"

"I'd enjoy that very much."

* * *

Since they held chapel services at NLC on Sunday morning, Connie didn't often attend church with her parents, and she welcomed the opportunity to worship with Joseph—it would be the first time they'd gone to church together. The congregation was a new fellowship, one her parents had helped organize three years ago. While they raised funds to erect a building, the congregation had purchased a Quonset hut for their meetings, which would be used as a gymnasium when they could afford a new sanctuary.

Connie was very conscious of Joseph as he sat between her and Beverly. They had refrained from touching for so many weeks that when she rubbed shoulders with him on the crowded pews, her heart overflowed with love for him. Were his senses responding to her in the same way? She thought it must be so, for with his arms crossed in front of him, he gently pinched her forearm. Startled, she glanced at him, and he smiled warmly, and the look in his eyes spoke loudly of his love for her. For a precious moment, they were secluded on an imaginary island, but the enchantment dissipated when the minister announced the number of the first hymn.

The simplicity of the building and its furnishings didn't detract from the warmth of the worship. The preacher—a senior citizen who'd come out of retirement to help organize the new fellowship—took his text from the book of Philippians: "And the peace of God, which transcends all understanding, will guard your hearts and your minds in Christ Jesus."

How unusual that the minister used the same text that Connie had read a few nights ago! She hoped that the words would also bring assurance to Joseph's heart, as it had to hers.

Joseph focused on the words *transcends all understanding*. In spite of his uncertain future, it amazed him that the peace of God flooded his soul this morning. During the closing hymn, at the invitation of the preacher, Joseph went forward to pray.

As he knelt on the concrete floor, Connie appeared beside him and slipped her hand into his. Speaking lowly, so that no one could hear except Connie, he prayed, "God, thank you for the peace of mind that I have this morning. I can't understand why You love me enough to be concerned about my affairs, but I believe You are. The next few days may be crucial for my happiness, and Connie's. Please help me to focus on You and Your promise, 'if You're for me, who can be against me.' Amen."

As soon as Joseph started heading his pickup northeast out of Denver, Connie said, "I finally hit pay dirt on that clipping. I had an e-mail message last night from a newspaper in a small southern California town. Two people were involved in the holdup, and although they both wore ski masks, the clerk thought one of them was a woman because of her petite body, slender, well-formed hands and the turquoise necklace she was wearing. It's possible there was a third person driving the getaway car."

"Then it could have been Virginia, the necklace implicates her and she did have shapely hands and she took care of them. I'd hoped she'd want to have a flower garden at the ranch, for I've never had time for that, and I like flowers, but she wasn't about to dirty her hands in the soil." He smiled wryly. "It's obvious I didn't know much about the woman I married. What else did you learn?"

"The robbers didn't get much money, but they cleaned out the drug department."

"It's inconceivable that a lethargic, shy woman like Virginia could ever be involved in a holdup, but if she had an addiction, she might have done most anything. No doubt that's why she was kept in close confinement in her home for several months." Joseph hit the steering wheel with his hand. "I still find it hard to forgive George and his parents for not telling me that. If I'd known she had a history of addiction, I would have tried to stop her alcohol consumption."

Connie laid a hand on his shoulder. "The past few months, I've often repeated the words of the Apostle Paul, 'Forgetting what is behind and straining toward what is ahead, I press on.' Don't allow the past to blight your future. You'll be able to put it behind you when you sort out what happened to your wife." Connie forced herself to acknowledge the fact that Virginia had been his wife. As much as it hurt, she would have to live with that knowledge the rest of her life. She couldn't be jealous of what had happened before she met Joseph.

He squeezed her hand. "I know. It hurts much more when a friend betrays you."

"Jesus was betrayed by one of His closest friends, and He forgave."

"And I will, too, eventually." He slowed for the exit to Brighton. "Did you find out anything else?"

"That one of the robbers was apprehended two

months ago and charged with the crime, but he won't give any information about the second party."

He took his eyes off the road for a minute. "Well, that is a breakthrough! Maybe we can prove something after all."

Joseph pulled a card from his pocket. "These are the directions I got. Check and see if I'm going in the right direction. I'm not familiar with Brighton."

"I believe you turn right on the next street," Connie said after she scanned the directions.

They were in a housing development of elaborate homes on large lots, most of them surrounded by stone walls. "It looks as if Debbie has done pretty well for herself. She was a friend Virginia picked up at college, and if I remember, her family had a medium income. Mrs. Perry wasn't pleased with the friendship."

"If you'll excuse me for saying so, you must not have been on Virginia's social scale either."

"No, not at all, and I wondered why they would favor our marriage. Now that I'm beginning to understand why, I'm not sure it's any credit to me."

"Oh, I think you should be flattered. They wanted Virginia to marry an upstanding, clean-cut guy who'd take her away from her former friends, preferably out of the city, and guide her in a different direction."

"Perhaps you're right. I'm sorry it didn't work out."

"The problem lay in her past—it had nothing to do with you."

He paused in front of a three-story stone house. "This must be it."

A woman in her midthirties with bleached hair, a

terrific tan and hard brown eyes opened the door soon after Joseph rang the bell. If she was disturbed by their presence, she hid it well.

"Well, Joseph Caldwell! What a surprise," the woman said, her words tumbling out rapidly.

"Hello, Debbie. This is my friend, Connie Harmon. May we come in?"

"Certainly, Joseph. It's been a long time since we've met."

She invited them to sit in a small living room to the left of the entrance hall. "May I get you something to eat? A cola or lime crush?"

Connie shook her head, and Joseph said, "No, thank you. We had a large dinner not long ago."

"I haven't heard anything about you lately," Debbie said. "I didn't know if you were in jail or still in the hospital. The newspapers indicated you'd suffered a serious injury."

"My injury was serious, but thanks to Connie, who operates a therapy center near Idaho Springs, I'm walking again."

"Glad to hear it. Now what can I do for you?"

"From your comment, you obviously know that I'm a suspect in Virginia's death. *I* know I'm innocent, and now that I'm well again, I intend to prove it by investigating the circumstances leading up to her death. I believe you have information that can help me find a solution to the mystery."

"I'm certainly willing to help you, but I don't know how I can. I haven't seen Virginia for over three years, and except for a Christmas card or two, I've had no contact with her since I moved to California."

"I don't want information about her after we were

married—it's the years before I knew her that I'm investigating. As her closest friend, you should know quite a lot, especially the year the two of you traveled together.''

Debbie offered them a cigarette. When they declined, she took one from the package and tapped it on the table. Connie detected a slight tremor in her hand as she flicked a lighter and held it to the cigarette. Her hard brown eyes didn't reveal anything, but she drew deeply on the cigarette and exhaled smoke through her nostrils before she answered.

"Really, Joseph! You don't expect me to tell you everything we did. We did the usual things anyone does when they're bumming around the country. What Virginia did before you were married isn't any of your business.''

"It is if it had anything to do with her death, and I believe that her death, if it wasn't accidental, was triggered by her past.'' He took the newspaper clipping and beach photo from his pocket. "What can you tell me about either of these?''

She glanced at the two items, and carelessly dropped the clipping on the table. "I've never seen that before. But obviously that's me in the picture. We were on a beach somewhere.''

"Who's the man with you and Virginia?''

"A cousin of mine. He traveled with us part of the time.''

"What's his name?''

"Stan Jarvis.'' Debbie threw down the photo angrily. "What difference does it make? I can assure you that Stan wasn't around here when Virginia was killed, and although this might wound your male ego,

Stan knew Virginia long before you did. He used to visit her when her parents were away."

That cleared up the identity of Virginia's unknown visitor that Rose had mentioned, Joseph decided.

Connie nudged Joseph's foot with the toe of her shoe, and he looked at her quickly. "According to my e-mail message, Stan Jarvis is the suspect apprehended in that pharmacy holdup."

Debbie's face flamed with anger, and she turned on Connie. "Who are you anyway? A detective?"

"I'm Joseph's friend and physical therapist, and I'm interested in proving his innocence. Our Center is dedicated to the healing of the whole body. Joseph won't heal completely until he's no longer suspected of a crime."

"All the pieces are beginning to fall into place," Joseph said, and his gray eyes glinted with anger. "Jarvis was your husband's name. Are you sure this guy is your cousin?"

"I might as well tell you, to save you the trouble of finding out what's common knowledge. Stan and I *are* distant cousins, but I married him four years ago, and divorced him last year."

"So the three of you held up that pharmacy. Virginia and Stan went inside, and you drove the getaway car. It all fits into place."

Debbie bounded out of her chair, and her voice shook until her words were almost unintelligible. "I don't like your insinuations. None of us were near that pharmacy the day of the holdup."

"The police must think that Stan was, or they wouldn't have arrested him."

"Police have been known to make mistakes. But

if you think you can manufacture an alibi for yourself by pinning Virginia's death on Stan, think again. He was in a San Francisco hospital the whole month of January this year, and if I remember right, Virginia was killed in January. I learned about it when I got back from Hawaii, where I was vacationing in January, so both Stan and I have airtight alibis for the day Virginia died." She motioned them toward the door. "Get out of here, and don't bother me again. I hope they put you in prison and throw away the key."

Connie felt like a dog must feel when it had been whipped, as she crawled back into the truck with Joseph. His eyes were wretched, and he said, as he backed out of the driveway, "I'm sorry you had to experience that, Connie. I don't know why you put up with me—I've given you nothing but trouble."

She managed a light laugh. "This is the second time in so many days we've been asked to leave a house, so I'm getting used to it. But, Joseph, I'm getting scared. I'm not sure we should be doing this ourselves. Like George Perry, Debbie knows more than she's telling, and if she was involved in that robbery, she'll try to stop you from learning anything else. Why don't you take the facts you have and turn them over to the authorities? Stan Jarvis's trial is scheduled for next month, and the information you have might secure his conviction."

"I don't know enough to interest the police yet, but I agree there could be some danger, and I don't want you involved. I'll continue the investigation on my own."

"I'm already involved, and I'll keep searching as long as you do."

He pulled into the parking lot of a grocery store. "Let's stop here and consolidate what information we have. If Stan was in the hospital when Virginia was killed, and I believe Debbie was telling the truth, then Virginia's fall was an accident, or another person was involved."

"Are we overlooking something important?"

"Possibly. I still think Virginia's problems are connected to that holdup. Although Stan can't be implicated in Virginia's death, he could have blackmailed her, for her last cash withdrawal was in November. And except for some joint securities she held with George that she couldn't touch, she had nothing left."

"Perhaps Debbie is the one who did the blackmailing. I couldn't help wondering where she'd gotten the money to buy that house. You said her family wasn't wealthy."

"There's no doubt in my mind that it was built with Virginia's inheritance. I think the reason Stan won't tell the authorities about Virginia's involvement is that he doesn't want his name connected with hers because that could also lead to a blackmail charge. It may be that both Debbie and Stan conspired to blackmail Virginia, and probably got married so they wouldn't have to testify against each other. The thing that galls me is why Virginia didn't tell me. I was naive enough to believe we didn't keep any secrets from each other. How wrong I was!"

"Didn't you talk about the past?"

"I didn't pry into her life before we were married—I assumed that she'd done nothing that concerned our marriage. Besides, we didn't talk a lot. Virginia was quiet and reserved."

"It's difficult to believe that kind of person would hold up a pharmacy."

"I've heard the old adage, still waters run deep. So who knows what Virginia was really like? That's what I like about you, Connie. You're easy to talk to. I don't think we'll ever run out of subjects to discuss." He lifted her hand to kiss it, praying for the day when he could open his heart to her. He wouldn't ask her to commit to a lifetime together until his record was wiped clean.

"What's your next move?" Connie asked.

"I'll take you back to the Center, and after I've had a few days to sort out what I know, I'll talk to my lawyers. Now that it seems reasonable that Debbie and Stan were involved, it shouldn't be impossible to find out if they received any money. In the meantime, I want you to be watchful. I may have tangled you in a dangerous situation."

"*You* be careful! You have an enemy in Debbie Smith Jarvis."

"Apparently she's been my enemy for quite a while, and I had no idea. Now that I know, I'll be wary of her."

Connie moved close to Joseph and laid her hand on his shoulder as they drove back to the church where she'd left the van.

They didn't talk much. Connie was concerned about Joseph, and how this proof of his wife's unsavory past had wounded his pride. Had she been unfaithful to him after they were married? If she wondered about it, how much more the possibility must weigh on Joseph's mind.

Joseph was trying to think how he could protect

Connie if this investigation became dangerous. He also questioned if he should even continue their relationship with a scandal looming over his head.

When he drove into the church parking lot, empty except for Connie's van, he pulled her into his arms and squeezed her so tight that she found it hard to breathe, but she didn't protest. Even yet she didn't dare tell him how much she loved him, but she whispered, "You're very special to me, Joseph. No matter what happens, you can count on me."

His eyes were misty when he released her and placed a tender kiss on her lips.

Chapter Twelve

Connie hadn't expected to hear from Joseph for several days, but he telephoned her the next night.

"Can we meet for dinner tomorrow night?" he asked. "I hate to ask since I told you to separate yourself from my dilemma, but something else has come up that I want to discuss with you."

"I can't leave NLC tomorrow evening because several of the staff members will be in Denver for some required training, and I need to stick around. But we can talk here. Come early enough for dinner."

"We're cutting alfalfa now, so I probably won't get away that early, but I'll be there."

Connie puzzled all the next day over Joseph's call because he sounded troubled, and when he arrived at eight o'clock, she noted his concern immediately. He even limped slightly, and she knew mental stress aggravated his injury.

"Let's walk down to the lake," he said. "I don't want our conversation to be overheard. I know I said

I'd keep you out of my problems, but I'm really disturbed about what I've discovered.''

After they arrived at the lake and sat on the stone bench, he hesitated several minutes before pulling a cigarette lighter from his pocket and handing it to her.

George Perry, Christmas Day, was inscribed on the gold-plated lighter.

She turned the object over in her hand, and looked at Joseph speculatively.

''I found the lighter under a chair cushion in our living room. It's where I sit when I watch television, and,'' he grinned, ''last night I was having a snack and overturned a glass of cola in the chair. When I was cleaning up the mess, my hand encountered a hard object wedged in the back side—this lighter.''

Favoring him with a feigned disapproving glare, Connie said, ''Outside of the fact that you've admitted to snacking before bedtime, what else is significant?''

''Virginia gave that lighter to George last Christmas at the Perry house. George and Stephanie left for two weeks' vacation to Florida the day after Christmas. They didn't return until the evening before Virginia was killed.''

Connie's eyes widened. ''Are you suggesting George was at the ranch the day of the tragedy?''

''He must have been. I was home all evening the night before the accident, so he wasn't there then. But I was out all the next morning helping to drive the Charolais in close to the barns before the blizzard struck. By the time I came home in midafternoon, there were several inches of snow on the ground. Any automobile tracks would have been obliterated.''

"This is terrible! What are you going to do?"

"I'll have to confront George with what I've learned. I can't believe that he would injure his sister, or if he did, that he'd drive off and leave her to die. But if he was there, why doesn't he say so, and why is he so keen to blame me? I've got to know."

"When are we going to see him?"

Joseph shook his head. "*You're* not going. After the way he treated us on our first visit, I won't subject you to that again."

Connie put her arms around him. "It's difficult for you to lose a friend as well as your wife, and I won't have you confront him alone. You might need a witness. If our roles were reversed, wouldn't you want to go with me?"

He moved closer, leaned over and kissed her.

"You win. When will it be convenient for you to go?"

"Thursday evening. Will you notify him that we're coming?"

"No, I think not. If he does have a guilty conscience, that would give him time to manufacture an alibi."

As they walked away from the lake, Joseph said, "Do you suppose Rose had any food left from dinner? I didn't have time to eat."

"Joseph!" she reproached him. "A bedtime snack last night, and no dinner today. You *must* eat regular meals."

"I need a woman to take care of me and see that I have good food to eat," he said pointedly.

"Then you'll have to marry Rose or Mom. They're the only good cooks I know. Come on. Rose has probably gone to her room, but I have a key to the kitchen. We'll find something for you.''

So that Joseph wouldn't have to leave his haying operation early on Thursday, Connie drove into Denver to meet him. He didn't voice his appreciation for her presence, but he squeezed her hand tightly when she settled into the truck beside him.

''I just hope they're home,'' Joseph said, as they walked up on the porch of the Perry home. ''I've dreaded this visit so much that I wouldn't want to go through such trauma another day.''

The same maid who'd admitted them the week before opened the door. Apparently Joseph didn't think she'd remember him, for he identified himself.

''I'm Joseph Caldwell. Will you ask Mr. Perry if he'll see me? Tell him Miss Harmon is with me.''

The woman closed the door, and Connie wondered if they'd be left standing on the steps. A few minutes later, George opened the door.

''Come in. We're in the library.'' He didn't offer to shake hands with either of them, and his face was unreadable. If their visit angered him, Connie couldn't tell from his facial expression.

Stephanie sat with embroidery in her hands, and she greeted them cordially, but without much warmth, which Connie deduced was her normal manner. ''Sit down,'' she invited. Connie took a seat on a chair near the door.

''I've come on an unpleasant errand,'' Joseph said, ''so I'll stand to say what I must. George, a few nights ago, I found the cigarette lighter Virginia gave you for Christmas beneath a chair cushion in my living room. You could only have left it there the day Virginia was killed. I'd like an explanation, please."

Stephanie gasped and half rose from her chair, staring at her husband. George turned his back on Joseph and started out of the room.

"After what your accusation has put me through the past nine months, you owe me an explanation," Joseph said.

Without answering, George left the room, and Stephanie ran after him. "Do something, Joseph," she shouted. "He hasn't been like himself since Virginia's death. I've been worried about him." She stopped in the doorway and wrung her hands, as George returned holding an envelope in his hand.

"Sit down, all of you," he said wearily. "I might have known, Joseph, that you wouldn't give up until you learned the truth. First of all, let me tell you that whatever happened between Virginia and me was an accident. I would never have harmed my sister deliberately."

Connie went to Joseph and they sat together on a couch facing George's chair. He held her hand until it hurt, but she didn't protest.

George's hands trembled, and he pulled a sigh from deep within. "It will be a relief to get this off my mind," he said in a raspy voice. "I realized that Virginia had lived a wild life while she was away from home that year, but I didn't know any details. I should have told you about it before you were married, but I really didn't think it would make any difference to you, and that it would be easier for both of you if you didn't know."

"Yes. I would have married her, but if I'd been

aware of her problems, I could have encouraged her to straighten up her life.''

"Right before Christmas," George continued in a trembling voice, "Virginia started pestering me to sell some of the stocks that we held jointly, and we had several quarrels about it. I had no idea why she wanted the money, so I refused. Upon her death, all of those stocks came to me, and that would have cast suspicion on me if anyone knew I was at the ranch when she fell. That's why I hid that fact."

Behind them, Connie heard Stephanie sniffling, so she went to her, perched on the arm of the chair where she huddled, holding her face in her hands. Connie laid a tender hand on her shoulder.

"I had no idea Virginia was being blackmailed," George continued, "nor why, but the night we got back from Florida, this letter was waiting for me." He passed it to Joseph. "Read it."

Joseph took the letter out of the envelope, and a newspaper clipping fell out—it was identical to the one Rose had found.

Joseph scanned the message and then read it aloud.

To George Perry:
For the sum of $50,000, I'll forget the name of the woman pictured here. It would be too bad to blacken the reputation of one of Colorado's most upstanding families. Get the money in cash, and I'll be in touch by telephone.

He handed the message back to George. "Did you pay the money?"

"No one ever telephoned me, or I might have. I

was sure the smaller person in the picture was Virginia, but before I got over my fear and anger about that, my broker telephoned. He's Virginia's broker, too, and since Virginia allowed me to handle all her investments, I thought I had the right to know, so I asked him point-blank about the status of Virginia's account. He told me she'd been withdrawing large amounts of money since Father died, and she had nothing left. I knew then that she'd been blackmailed.''

Joseph got up and walked across the room, staring out the window at the floodlit fountain casting its sparkling spray high in the air. Connie figured his thoughts were so troubled that he didn't even see the water. George spoke in a monotone, but quickly, as if he were at last facing the reality of what had happened that day at the ranch.

"In spite of the approaching blizzard, I drove to the ranch. Virginia was alone in the house, and we had a terrific quarrel. She admitted to the robbery, and to being blackmailed, too. She said now that her money was gone she feared he would start on me, and that's the reason she sent me that note, so I'd be forewarned. In the scuffle, she stepped backward, tripped over the rug in front of the fireplace, fell heavily, and struck her head on that bronze sculpture. I dialed 911, but the line was dead. Virginia's head was bleeding, and I panicked. I hurried out to my car and left.''

George dropped his head into his hands, wailing, "If that fall killed her, it was an accident. It was an accident! You believe me, don't you Joseph?''

George started pacing the floor, and Joseph went to him and embraced him. "Yes, I believe you."

Stephanie lifted her head and looked at the two men, and with an effort, or so it seemed to Connie, she went to her husband.

"Come, George," she said quietly. "Sit down. We must decide what to do."

She pulled him beside her on the couch, and Joseph sat on his other side. "There's only one thing I can do, Stephanie. I'll go to the police and tell them the whole story." He turned to Joseph. "I can't tell you how sorry I am that I threw suspicion on you."

Joseph's overwhelming relief that the mystery was solved at last, and that he'd been exonerated from suspicion of Virginia's death was overshadowed by his sympathy for George.

He put an arm over George's trembling shoulders. "I'm sorry too, that you've been carrying this burden alone. Straighten up now, and we'll see what we can do."

Connie and Joseph exchanged glances and she threw him a kiss. They could rejoice later.

"The man involved with her in that robbery," Joseph said, "has apparently been blackmailing Virginia. He's Stan Jarvis, Debbie Smith's cousin—and former husband—who traveled with Virginia and Debbie a lot. Debbie may have been the intermediary, but in that note, Virginia said 'he,' so she didn't suspect Debbie's involvement. Stan has been arrested and jailed for the crime, and his trial comes up next month. Connie and I have been doing a lot of investigating, and I'm inclined to believe that Debbie was also involved in the holdup, driving the getaway vehicle. She's living in a house that she couldn't possibly have paid for. So we figure she and her former husband were both in the blackmailing. My lawyers are trying to trace the money to them.''

"Are you going to sue to get the money back?" Stephanie asked.

"No. I'll go with you to the police, and tell them my suspicions. All I want is for my name to be cleared. If they prove Debbie and her husband got the money, George can sue for it if he wants to. It's Perry money, and I don't want any of it. I'm making my own way.''

Gripping George's shoulder hard, Joseph stood. "What time do you want me to return in the morning?" he asked.

With pleading eyes, Stephanie looked at him. "Stay here tonight, Joseph. George may need you."

Perhaps Stephanie feared that George might harm himself, for Joseph agreed immediately. "I'll take Connie back to where we left her car, and I should be back in a half hour." He leaned over and embraced George again. "I'll stand by you, old friend."

Joseph's eyes were wet when he and Connie walked down the hall.

"I don't want you to stay here, Joseph," she said when they reached the truck. "They may still be your enemies, and if so, your life could be in danger tonight."

"I don't think so, but it's a risk I have to take. It was hard for me to forgive George for what he put me through, but I have, and I want to help him all I can."

"Will charges be filed against him?"

"I doubt it. He'll take the family lawyers with us, and they'll probably get him released on probation. Actually, he didn't commit a crime, for if that blow did kill Virginia, it was accidental. Of course, they were fighting, but Virginia would have been as much at fault as George. Sometimes people are charged with involuntary manslaughter in such a situation, but we'll have to wait for tomorrow to see."

"Will you ever know what caused Virginia's death?"

"I doubt it, and I suppose it doesn't matter which way she died. When I'm no longer suspected of any crime in that connection, I'll try to put it behind me."

Joseph drew Connie into his arms when they reached the NLC van. "Don't worry about me, and be careful driving home. In a few days, we'll have a long, serious talk."

He kissed Connie, and squeezed her so hard that she gasped. Joseph released her reluctantly, went with her to the van, and assured himself that the locks were secured. Watching her drive away, he breathed a prayer for her safety. He couldn't lose her, too, for he knew without a doubt how indispensable she was to his happiness. In his heart he'd known for a long time that he loved her, but he couldn't tell her when there was a possibility he might go to prison. His love for Virginia had grown cold a long time ago, but she still cast a shadow between him and Connie. With a sigh, he turned back to his truck. He dreaded tomorrow's events. He wished he could have proven his innocence without embarrassing George, but apparently that wouldn't be possible.

* * *

All the next day Connie thought of Joseph and wondered how traumatic the experience would be. In her imagination, she followed the Perrys and Joseph as they left their home, went to the police station and were subjected to questioning. She had asked Kim to hold all telephone calls, and to ward off any visitors. So she was surprised when shortly before noon, Kim's voice came over the intercom, "You have a visitor, Connie. I think you should see him."

She agreed, but was ill prepared to have Ray Blazer open the door and walk into her office.

She half rose from her chair, and then sat down again. Ray walked slowly to her desk. She was still afraid of him, and she was glad he hadn't closed the door between her office and Kim's. She had nothing to say to Ray, so she waited for him to speak first.

"I'm leaving for California," he said, "and I've come to apologize for the trouble I caused you."

"I accept your apology," she said. In her heart she was happy that he'd come. She hadn't been pleased with her unforgiving spirit toward Ray, and with his sincere apology, she was able to forgive him completely. After all, Ray didn't have the grace of God to prevent him from taking what he wanted without regard for others.

"I hadn't been raised in the type of home you'd had, and moral license was common among my people," he explained. "I did love you, Connie, and I thought your Marriage First vow was foolish. I learned different when I lost you because I refused to recognize that pledge. I know it's too late now, but I do wish things could have worked out for us."

Connie stood, and her knees trembled slightly. She

shook her head. "We wouldn't have been happy together, Ray. I see that now, but I had many miserable days after I broke our engagement. I sincerely hope you'll find someone else who will make you happier than I ever could."

"Have you found someone else?" he asked pointedly.

"I don't know. I do love Joseph, and he loves me, but until his name is cleared of suspicion over his wife's death, there's no future for us. Both of us realize that."

"I hope you do find happiness with Caldwell. You're a wonderful woman, Connie, and you deserve it. Tell him to check into his wife's past. I'd known Virginia..." and when Ray saw the astonished look on Connie's face, he hastened to add, "Oh, don't get me wrong—there was nothing between us. We were in college together, and although she seemed to be a timid, quiet person, she dated some wild characters. If she was murdered, some of those guys could have done it."

"Thank you, Ray."

She held out her hand, and he took it, holding it longer than Connie liked, and she wondered if he had indeed loved her. Releasing her hand, she said, "Goodbye, Ray, and best wishes for the future. I mean that. You're a great physical therapist."

He spoke briefly to Kim as he left the office, and Connie knew that Ray at last had gone from her life. Whether or not she would tell Joseph what he'd said, she didn't know. It seemed every place they turned, a different aspect of Virginia's character emerged.

* * *

When Joseph telephoned at five o'clock, the pressure of the day was evident by the weariness of his voice.

"Well, it's all over, Connie," he said.

"Oh, Joseph, my dear, was it bad?"

"Dreadful for George and Stephanie, and I suffered for them. It will all be on the television news tonight."

"Where are you?"

"At the ranch. I wanted to come and see you, tell you in person, but there was an emergency with some of the cattle, and I came home. We had to have a vet, and he's just now finished. I want to see you, but I'm about drained."

"I'll come to you," Connie said. "I can be there in a couple of hours, and I'll see if Rose can provide some food for our dinner."

"That's a long drive if you go back tonight. Bring some overnight things, and I'll ask Jean to spend the night here. She's coming to the ranch later on, for she's anxious to know what happened today, too."

Connie stopped in the outer office long enough to tell Kim about Joseph's call and that she was leaving for the night. Within a half hour, she was on her way to Joseph. Were they at the end of the long road?

The time passed more quickly than Connie anticipated, for her mind was busy with thoughts of the future. Was Joseph ready for another relationship? Would he ever be? Had Virginia's death, and the traumatic events that followed, scarred him so deeply that he would be reluctant to ever give his love freely to another? And if they were to marry, would she have to give up her therapy work to live at the ranch? Joseph needed a wife in his home, not one who worked a hundred miles away. She couldn't expect him to give up his ranch—his livelihood—to live near NLC, so Connie knew that she would have to make a choice—Joseph or the NLC. Since God had called her to minister in His name as a physical therapist, was it right to give up that ministry to marry Joseph? Throughout the drive, Connie pondered questions that had no easy answers. But it might soon be crunch time.

Joseph came to the car and took Connie in his arms when she stepped out of the van. He held her a long time without speaking. "It's over, Connie. I couldn't speak of this until I'd proven my innocence in Virginia's death, but I've loved you for months. I agree with you that the test of love is a wedding ring, and I want to put one on your finger as soon as possible. Will you marry me?"

Kissing him, she said lovingly, "Of course, I've been waiting for you to ask."

With his arm still around her, they walked into the house. "You'll never know how much I appreciate you coming here," he said. "I couldn't bear to spend the evening without seeing you, but I didn't know if I could make the trip to NLC."

She ran her fingers over the lines in his face, etched deeply by distress. "Let's have our dinner," she said, "and you'll feel better. Help me carry in the food. We can warm it in the microwave."

"Jean will be here in an hour or so. She had a meeting in Fort Collins this evening."

After they'd eaten, they sat on the couch in the

living room. Joseph drew Connie close, and she curled up in the circle of his arm. "Now, tell me everything," she said.

"There really isn't so much to tell. After the turmoil of the past months, today was anticlimactic." He paused for a few moments, perhaps reflecting on the day's activities. "I didn't sleep any last night," he continued, "and I don't suppose George and Stephanie did either. We were all up early for breakfast, but none of us ate much."

"I'm happy that you and George are friends again. I believe his disloyalty caused you more grief than anything else."

"That's true," Joseph agreed. "But back to this morning. We met his lawyers at the police station near the Perry home. George made a clean breast of everything. He submitted the blackmail note, told them about his trip to the ranch, how he and Virginia had quarreled and about her fall. I gave them all the facts you and I have gathered about Stan and Debbie Jarvis, and that holdup. They weren't happy that we'd been investigating privately." He chuckled. "I told them that we wouldn't have had to investigate if they'd believed me and had done their own detective work."

"That must have given you a great deal of satisfaction," Connie said.

"As a matter of fact, it did," he said, laughing. "I resent being considered guilty without any proof."

"So what happens now?"

"George won't be charged with anything—they reluctantly accepted his story that her fall was accidental, and since she was alive when I found her, the official report will probably be death from an injury sustained in an accident.''

"What about Debbie Jarvis? Will she be implicated?"

Joseph nodded. "The local police are already in touch with the authorities in California about the holdup, and I feel sure that Debbie will also be arrested."

"How are George and Stephanie? This must be terrible for them."

"George seems more relieved than anything else. He's been miserable for months—worrying that he may have been responsible for Virginia's death and being sorry that he'd implicated me. We both did a lot of apologizing and forgiving today. He's so happy he has a clear conscience now that he won't mind all the publicity. The Perrys have been influential in this area for years, and Stephanie's father has a lot of political clout, but the local media might go easy on them." He sighed. "It's over now, and I can go forward. That brings me to us. When can we be married?"

"Joseph, I've been wondering about that during my drive to the ranch, for I thought you might ask me, and I believe we should wait for a while. These past few months have wounded you, emotionally and physically, and you need time to heal. How would a six months' engagement sound to you?"

"Too long!" he groaned. "But I know you're right. We should carry on a normal courtship, when we could talk about something else besides my physical and legal problems. Let's be romantic and get married on the anniversary of the day we met at NLC—that would be on May 5.''

"Why, Joseph," Connie said, with an impish grin. "You even remember the exact date! I hadn't taken you for a romantic!"

"I haven't had much of a chance," he complained. "Just wait until I *really* turn on my charm, and you won't be disappointed." He stood and pulled Connie upward into his arms. "I hear Jean coming up the driveway, so let me give you a *real* kiss before she gets here."

He did, and Connie wasn't disappointed.

Epilogue

Connie's heart—and her lips—sang as she left NLC's administration building to prepare for her wedding. She locked the door with some regret. For not only was this her last day as a single woman, but she was closing the Center today. She and Joseph had delayed their marriage for a whole year after their engagement, while she built an elaborate health spa on a twenty-acre corner of his ranch. They had agreed that she must continue her therapy work, but in the vicinity of Fort Collins. She'd been fortunate to find a buyer for NLC, and the new owners would take over tomorrow and operate the property as a resort, which it had been intended for in the beginning.

Most of her staff was moving to Fort Collins, and Connie eventually intended to broaden the scope of her ministry to hold conferences on the relationship between physical health and spiritual growth.

Since Connie and Joseph had met at NLC, they wanted to have the ceremony there, and the lawn behind the administration building was decorated much as it had been when Kim and Eric had been married. Today, Eric would be performing the ceremony. They had only two attendants. Kim was the matron of honor, while George Perry served as Joseph's best man. During the past year, Connie and Joseph had often visited the Perrys, and Connie and Stephanie had become good friends. George looked with favor upon Joseph's marriage to Connie.

Wearing a sparkling white wedding gown to symbolize her belief in the Marriage First vow that she'd promoted, Connie took her father's arm and started up the flower-bordered aisle toward Joseph. A worry-free year had erased the lines from his face, and it had been months since she'd noted any despair in his gray eyes. He looked happy! For a moment, Connie wondered if he was comparing this simple ceremony to the ostentatious wedding when he'd married Virginia, but she shoved the thought aside. The year had also erased the hold Virginia held in his thoughts, and she had no doubt that Joseph loved her as much or more than he had his first wife.

Bill Harmon delivered Connie to the makeshift altar and placed her hand in Joseph's strong one. Eric followed the traditional wedding service, with one exception. Before the giving and receiving of rings, he added one additional vow. He read the Marriage First pledge and asked if they had obeyed the pledge. In unison, they said, "We did," and repeated, "I believe my body is the temple of the Holy Spirit. If I defile my body with immorality, I dishonor the Spirit of God living within me. Therefore, I pledge to maintain the purity of my body until my wedding day."

As Peggy McCane sang, "With this Ring I Thee Wed," Joseph placed a wide golden band on Connie's finger.

"We did it!" he whispered. "We passed the test of love."

* * * * *

Dear Reader,

The concept of the program at the New Life Center—that a healthy body and a pure soul complement each other—is one of my basic beliefs. I've been a Christian since I was eleven years old, so I learned as a child that my body was the dwelling place of the Holy Spirit. Several years ago my husband and I committed to a lifestyle of exercise, a healthy diet and self-discipline to keep our bodies the kind of place where the Holy Spirit can live and work through us. Now that we're healthy senior citizens, we recognize the wisdom of that decision. I like to cook and bake, so we don't live on a starvation diet, but we eat most foods in moderation.

And since I mentioned a chocolate pecan pie several times in this book, you might enjoy my recipe for this *calorie-filled,* delicious dessert that we enjoy on *rare* occasions.

3 eggs, slightly beaten
1 cup dark corn syrup
4 (4-oz) squares of semisweet chocolate, melted and cooled
$1/3$ cup sugar
2 tbsp butter or margarine, melted
1 tsp pure vanilla
$1^1/2$ cups chopped pecans
1 unbaked 9-inch pastry shell

Heat oven to 350°F. In a large bowl stir together eggs, corn syrup, chocolate, sugar, butter and vanilla until well blended. Stir in pecans and pour into pastry shell. Bake 50-60 minutes.

A few days ago I received a two-page letter from a reader who began, "I know you're too busy to answer my letter, but..." Authors thrive on fan mail—either positive or negative—so when anyone takes the time to write, I find the time to answer. If you'd like to write and receive my semiannual newsletter, my mailing address is P.O. Box 2770, Southside, WV 25187.

May God bless you.

Irene B. Brand

Love Inspired®

Heartwarming Inspirational Romance

Here's your opportunity to sample another work by

Irene Brand

#0-373-87101-5 **Tender Love** $4.50 U.S.☐ $5.25 CAN.☐

(limited quantities available)

TOTAL AMOUNT	$
POSTAGE & HANDLING	$
($1.00 for one book, 50¢ for each additional)	
APPLICABLE TAXES*	$ _____
TOTAL PAYABLE	$ _____
(check or money order—please do not send cash)	

To order, send the completed form, along with a check or money order for the total above, payable to **Love Inspired,** to: **In the U.S.:** 3010 Walden Avenue, P.O. Box 9077, Buffalo, NY 14269-9077 **In Canada:** P.O. Box 636, Fort Erie, Ontario L2A 5X3.

Name: _____

Address: _____ City: _____

State/Prov.: _____ Zip/Postal Code: _____

Account # (if applicable): _____   075 CSAS

*New York residents remit applicable sales taxes.
  Canadian residents remit applicable GST and provincial taxes.